"I am going to be one hundred percent committed to our child. Do I make myself clear?"

Isobel swallowed.

"And one more thing." He set his jaw determinedly. "We will need to get married."

Orlando coldly watched the look of panic sweep over Isobel's face, the irony of the situation striking him. Never had he expected his marriage proposal to be met with such a reaction. But then, never had he expected to make one. Life as a single man had suited him just fine—he believed in working hard and taking his pleasures when and where he chose, usually in the form of beautiful women and always, always on his terms.

But circumstances had dramatically changed, the unimaginable had happened and now he was going to make Isobel his wife, no matter how distasteful she may find it. Because no way was he going to have his child growing up illegitimate, like he had. No way was he going to follow the pattern of his father in any shape or form.

Andie Brock

THE SHOCK CASSANO BABY

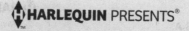
HARLEQUIN PRESENTS®

Recycling programs
for this product may
not exist in your area.

ISBN-13: 978-0-373-13911-8

The Shock Cassano Baby

First North American Publication 2016

Copyright © 2016 by Andie Brock

Printed in U.S.A.

Andie Brock started inventing imaginary friends around the age of four and is still doing that today; only now the sparkly fairies have made way for spirited heroines and sexy heroes. Thankfully she now has some real friends, as well as a husband and three children, plus a grumpy but lovable cat. Andie lives in Bristol and, when not actually writing, could well be plotting her next passionate romance story.

Books by Andie Brock

Harlequin Presents

The Sheikh's Wedding Contract
The Last Heir of Monterrato

Visit the Author Profile page
at Harlequin.com for more titles.

To my daughter Betsy.
For being an enthusiastic reader of my books
and encouraging her friends to be, too!
Love you, Bets.

CHAPTER ONE

ISOBEL STARED AT the figures on the screen one last time. The initial stages of the business plan had been implemented successfully; target forecasts were all on course. Yes, she was confident that the board of Cassano Holdings would be satisfied with the progress she had made so far. More than satisfied, even.

After closing the lid of her laptop Isobel zipped it into its case. She was ready. She glanced at her watch. There was just one more thing she had to do before she could leave for the board meeting in the city.

Rising to her feet, she smoothed down the skirt of her navy business suit and crossed the few steps to the sofa to pick up her handbag. Her heart was thumping now, her hand shaky as she slid it inside to retrieve the small packet in its chemist's bag.

Giving herself no more time to think she headed for the bathroom. There really was no going back.

'Any other business?'

Orlando Cassano leant back in his chair, the gold pen in his hand catching the light as it was slowly rotated by strong, olive-skinned fingers.

With a negative murmur the board members

started to gather together their papers, opening briefcases and stowing away their electronic devices.

'Isobel?' The dark sweep of his eyes now focussed directly on the young woman seated on the opposite side of the wide glass table. 'Is there anything else you want to add?'

'No.' Isobel shook her head. 'I think we have covered everything.'

If only that were true. Looking around, she forced herself to smile brightly at the assembled group of directors, accountants and marketing officers that comprised the UK division of Cassano Holdings. But there was no way she could meet the eye of the company CEO himself, whose piercing dark stare had been all over her ever since she had entered this boardroom and now, two hours later, still scorched across her skin. As if this wasn't hard enough, it seemed Orlando Cassano was intent on making it a whole lot worse.

'*Bene.* Then I think we can wrap this up for today.'

Orlando offered her a smile that knifed into her guts.

'You have done well, Isobel. I'm confident that this will be a rewarding partnership.' He paused, his brows knotting together as he watched the colour drain from her face.

'You've made a sound start, Ms Spicer, no doubt

about that.' The chief financial officer gave a nod of agreement. 'It's early days, but if you can replicate this performance I can see us renegotiating your contract sooner than anticipated.'

'That's good to know.' Isobel held on to her smile with grim tenacity. Six weeks ago, when she had signed the contract with Cassano Holdings, this news would have seen her skipping down the street. But now... Now it felt as if the world had tipped sideways and she was left clinging on to the edge.

Six weeks ago it had felt like a real gamble, signing over sixty per cent of her business to this massive corporate enterprise. But Spicer Shoes was expanding so rapidly it desperately needed a large injection of cash—and fast—and this was the only way Isobel had been able to think to do it.

She had been proud of her negotiating skills—securing the right to buy back twenty per cent of the shares and regain the all-important majority shareholding once the profit margins showed they could sustain it. In fact it had been easier than she'd thought.

But then so had falling into bed with the stunning Orlando Cassano.

Now, as she stared through the glass tabletop at the red suede ankle boot jiggling on her foot, she knew what a massive mistake that had been.

'Well, thank you, everybody.' Pushing himself

away from the table with the palms of his hands, Orlando waited, chivalry preventing him from standing before Isobel and the only other female present—a scarily efficient PA called Astrid—had done the same.

Finally the board members were filing out of the room, shaking Isobel's hand and politely congratulating her, their thoughts no doubt already turning to lunch.

And suddenly they were alone. Isobel's heart took up a thundering beat.

Orlando, tall and silent, stood with his back to the wall of windows, silhouetted against the London skyline. He looked dark and brooding and impossibly handsome, the elegant cut of his suit accentuating his considerable height and broad shoulders, the shirt white against his tanned skin. Isobel felt her throat go dry, her skin tighten against his imagined touch.

This was Orlando Cassano—a formidable businessman, a harder, colder, altogether more dangerous man than the one she had first met on the island of Jacamar. This was the man she had been prepared to meet when she had flown to his private Caribbean island to make her pitch for his company's investment in her business.

She had been such a bag of nerves then, but excited too, full of enthusiasm and ideas. Her business plan had been honed until it shone, her speech practised to perfection. Orlando Cassano was a tough nut to crack—everybody knew that. Legend had it that beneath his urbane good looks there lurked a heart of steel. But having secured the once-in-a-lifetime opportunity to meet him, through a client who happened to know him, there had been no way Isobel was going to mess it up.

Then she had met him…and all those preconceptions had vanished in a skyward-soaring heartbeat. Because the man she'd discovered on Jacamar had not been what she had been expecting at all. Arrestingly handsome, yes. But also relaxed, charming, funny. Not to mention deeply, bone-meltingly sexy.

She had noticed him straight away—how could she not have? From her seat on the little motorboat full of chattering staff she had watched the tall, commanding figure on the rickety landing stage coming closer into view. He'd been wearing faded board shorts and a sleeveless T-shirt, the breeze ruffling his dark curls, his feet bare on the sun-bleached wood. But even though he'd appeared to be someone who could undoubtedly rock the beach-bum look, Isobel had known immediately who he was. The confidence in his stance, the easy grace as he had stretched to catch the rope, the twinkle in his eye as it had caught hers—all had told her that this had to be the man she had come to see: billionaire businessman Orlando Cassano.

Isobel had waited as the other passengers disembarked, listening to their warm greetings as Orlando had helped them ashore, had assisted them with their parcels and packages, until finally it had been her turn. As she had wobbled to stand he had reached forward to take her hand, and the feel of that warm, firm grip against her skin had spread through her body like a bush fire. And it had burned there ever since...

'So, Ms Spicer.' Now, folding his arms across his broad chest, Orlando spoke. 'You are a surprisingly difficult woman to get hold of.'

His voice was low and deep, with just enough of an Italian accent to reveal his heritage and curl around Isobel's heart. But today there was no warmth to it.

'Why do I get the impression you have been avoiding me?'

'Not avoiding you.' Lifting her chin, Isobel took a second to bite down hard on her lip to stop it giving her away. 'I've just been busy, that's all. I thought that was what you wanted.'

'Busy is good. *Too* busy to answer my calls and emails, less so.' Moving away from the window Orlando strode over to the door to the outer office, closing it with a soft click before returning to stand a few feet in front of Isobel. 'I was beginning to worry.'

Isobel scanned his self-assured face for signs of

this so-called worry. Nothing. *But she was about to change all that*.

'Well, I hope the figures have shown you that everything is on track.' The slight tilt of his head, coupled with his narrowed eyes, suggested this was not the answer he was looking for, but Isobel pressed on. 'Full production is due to start in the factory in Le Marche very soon, and...'

'I'm not talking about the factory, Isobel, or the business—as well you know.' He closed the gap between them, his voice lethally calm. 'I'm talking about things on a more personal level. How about we start with my invitation to dinner that you have totally ignored?'

Isobel flinched. He was too close now, and she was faced with a besuited wall of taut muscle and towering height. He was messing with her ability to think clearly, to form sensible sentences.

It was true that she had ignored the email he had sent her last week. Well, *ignored* was hardly the right word—she had stared at it long and hard, trying to formulate a suitable reply, before eventually giving up. In any case, she strongly suspected that after she'd told him her news he would have a severe loss of appetite. She knew she did.

But it seemed that by failing to leap at the chance of spending an evening with him she had ruffled his feathers. In front of the board members he had been polite, professionally charming.

Now that politeness had turned to interrogation, and a cold stillness had settled over his handsome features—nothing like the impish devilment and sexy grin of the man she had known on Jacamar. No doubt somewhere there was a dent in that pristine pride of his—not that he would ever let her see it.

'I didn't reply to that email because I didn't think there was any point.'

Orlando's eyes narrowed further as he took a step closer to her. 'Go on.'

Isobel swallowed down the knot in her throat. 'I think that what happened on Jacamar…what we did… I mean…' She faltered beneath the mocking innocence of his gaze. 'I think from now on we should keep our relationship strictly professional.'

'Do you, indeed?'

Another step closer and the small space between them had vanished completely. Isobel felt her knees start to wobble.

'Yes—yes, I do.'

'And why is that, Ms Spicer?'

He placed his hands on her shoulders, warm and firm, nailing her to the ground. Now there was no escaping the physical, sexual tidal wave that was Orlando Cassano. No mistaking the raw throb of desire that pulsed between them, nor the answering roar of blood in her ears.

Isobel held herself very still, her arms by her

sides, determined to fight the intense feelings that were sweeping through her body. It would be so easy to raise her arms, link them around his neck, let herself be pulled against the taut strength of his body and satisfy the hunger she felt for him. But that way disaster lay—in fact it already had. No, she would take a second to compose herself, and then she would move away, do what she had to do.

But Orlando had other ideas about how to spend that second, and before she knew it his hands had moved to the back of her head, his fingers plundering the softness of her hair as he tipped her face up to his, seeking her lips with his own. His face blurred out of focus as he lowered his head to claim her, and suddenly he was kissing her, wasting no time before increasing the pressure and using the heated, erotic slide of his tongue to open her up to him.

It was a kiss full of heat and possessiveness and deep sexual need. A kiss that left no doubt as to where it would lead, if circumstances would let it. Isobel felt her eyes close against its force, her body instantly surrender to its power.

Orlando altered his position, sliding his leg against her thigh, pressing his arousal to her groin. 'I've missed you, Isobel.' He pulled his mouth away just far enough to groan the words against her swollen lips before angling his head in order to kiss her more deeply. Then, drawing in a deep breath he continued hoarsely, 'And I hope you have missed me too.'

'No!'

That split second of space was enough to bring Isobel to her senses and, bracing her hands against Orlando's chest, she used its rock-hard strength to push herself away. The look of surprise that flashed in his eyes cut through her like a blade.

'We have to stop this.'

Taking a step back, and then another, she fought to control the heaving of her chest, to stem the river of lust that was snaking its way to every part of her body.

'I mean, it's over—finished…' Her voice tailed off with the effort of dragging the reluctant words up from her body. From the absurdity of trying to reject the only man she had ever truly desired. 'We can't do this any more.'

Orlando tugged loose the tie that was suddenly unbearably tight around his neck and, shrugging off his jacket, hurled it behind him where it hooked limply over the back of a chair. It seemed nothing was going his way at the moment.

He had been looking forward to seeing Isobel again today—had been surprised, actually, just how much. Reacquainting himself with the lovely Ms Spicer was supposed to have been the one bright spot in what he knew was going to be a frustrating and depressing few days. Now it seemed even *that* pleasure was going to be denied him.

He'd allowed himself an extra day in London before he had to fly to Italy to sort out his late father's affairs. His business in the UK could be concluded pretty quickly, and the thought of spending some free time with Isobel had been a very attractive one. But, judging by the look on her face now, it was time that wasn't going to be needed. He might as well fly to Italy this evening, get it over with, then head back to New York as fast as his private jet would take him.

But it was a grim prospect. If he had his way he would never set foot in his home town of Trevente ever again. The ancient Italian town, sited between the turquoise waters of the Adriatic and the snow-capped Sibillini Mountains, had all the picture-postcard beauty you could ask for, but it certainly held no charm for Orlando. And as for the *castello* that looked down on the town, and the estate and the wretched title that went with it—Marchese di Trevente—well, he wanted none of it. Even if it *was* his rightful inheritance.

Some inheritance. Orlando felt a fresh wave of anger roll over him. Passed to him on the recent death of the miserable lowlife of a creature who had called himself his father, the once noble and profitable estate that had been in the Cassano family for countless generations had been brought to its knees, the vineyards neglected, the farms uncared for and the many properties virtually in ruins. And that included the majestic Castello Trevente.

This was his father's legacy—a legacy Orlando couldn't wait to get shot of. Finding out that he had to go to Trevente in person to do just that had only fuelled his rage. But despite putting his legal team on to it there appeared to be no way of circumnavigating the ancient Italian laws—no getting out of climbing the twisty stairs to the stuffy office of the family solicitor, shaking hands with notary, or the mayor, or whoever else had to witness his signature in this archaic system.

Only then would he be able to arrange for the sale of the whole damned place and finally walk away—wash his hands of his heritage for ever.

Now Orlando's eyes scanned the defiant figure who stood before him. So he was being dumped. There was a novelty value there, to be sure, but that didn't compensate for the sharp sting of rejection, the virtual slap on the cheek. Not to mention his disappointment that he was going to be denied a brief period of escapism with this lovely young woman.

The sensible thing would be to take Isobel's words at face value. Shake her hand and say goodbye. But his body was far from sensible where Ms Spicer was concerned. It had been from the very first moment he had seen her arrive on his Caribbean island, wobbling to stand up in the motor launch. Even now it was refusing to accept what he had been told, and the tightness in his groin was showing no sign of abating. He realised he wanted answers, *needed* answers, before he could walk away.

Isobel had retreated further from him now, deeper into the room, and she stared at him with something like mutinous rebellion. He watched as she pushed back her shoulders, tucking her glossy chestnut hair behind one ear. Her cheeks were stained with twin streaks of colour, her wide green eyes unnaturally bright. Something was going on here. And she wasn't leaving until he had damned well found out what it was.

Forcing himself to find some of the legendary calm that he was so famed for, Orlando moved over to the table and pulled out two chairs.

'Sit down, Isobel.'

Isobel hesitated, then did as she was told, crossing her legs and smoothing the short but sensible pencil skirt over her thighs. Seating himself opposite her, Orlando watched her top leg start to jiggle, and immediately his very male attention was drawn to the jut of her knee through the sheer tights, the graceful sweep of her calves down to those ankle boots with their vertiginously high heels.

He'd noticed them as soon as she had walked

into the boardroom—as had every other person sitting around that table. Their vivid red colour had flashed brighter than a robin's breast in the glass and steel setting of this modern office building.

Immediately his thoughts had flown to how he would remove them, sliding down the zippers at the side and inching them off her feet whilst Isobel was splayed across his bed, waiting for his attentions. That would work. Or maybe leaving them on, removing the rest of the clothes from her luscious body and waiting for those long legs to wrap around him, boots and all, with the suede rubbing against his skin, the scratch of the heels down his back.

Hearing Isobel clear her throat, he forced his way back to the present, his eyes back up to her heated face.

'So...' He leant back, stretching long legs out in front of him. 'Am I allowed to ask why the change of heart?'

Isobel shifted uncomfortably in her seat. 'It's not a change of heart.'

'What, then?'

He could see her struggling to find the right words. Her lips, he noticed, were still swollen from the force of their kiss—a kiss that had affected them both equally, no matter how much Isobel tried to cover it up.

'This is just for curiosity's sake, you understand.

I will obviously respect your decision, no matter what the reason.'

'I know that.'

'So…?' he repeated.

Goddammit, why didn't she have the guts just to come out with it? It wasn't as if he hadn't worked it out for himself by now anyway.

Impatience, and a possessiveness he didn't want to acknowledge, made his voice a growl. 'Perhaps you would like me to make it easier for you?'

At this, Isobel's green eyes shot up from where they had been watching her hands twisting in her lap. 'What do you mean?'

'You've met someone else.' Orlando was surprised by the way just saying those words made him want to go out and punch something—hard. 'A new boyfriend?'

'Ha!'

Isobel's bitter laugh, coupled with the look of astonishment on her face, told him he'd got that wrong and for a fleeting moment relief washed over him.

'Don't be ridiculous, Orlando.'

Was that so ridiculous? They hadn't seen each other for over a month. Plenty of time for some young gun to step in and claim Isobel for his prize. But it would seem that wasn't the case. Orlando's clenched fists loosened momentarily, before tightening again as another thought took hold.

'An old boyfriend, then?' His eyes narrowed, piercingly intense now as he waited for her answer. 'Perhaps someone you failed to mention when we were on Jacamar?'

'Of course not!' Isobel straightened her spine, tossing back her head so that the mane of hair gleamed richly. 'I would never have slept with you if I had had a boyfriend. What sort of a person do you take me for?'

Orlando shrugged. 'I don't know, Isobel, you tell me. Presumably not the same person I knew on Jacamar. Because *she* appeared to enjoy my company every bit as much as I did hers.'

'I *did*!' Her reply came out in a burst of anguish before she lowered her voice in soft confession. 'Of course I did.'

She turned her head to one side, but not before Orlando had caught sight of the flush of heat that had flooded her face. He waited, watching with cold interest as she struggled to find her composure.

'I'm not denying that what happened between us was…mutual.' The intensity of his gaze demanded more. 'Was…good, in fact. But that was in the past. Circumstances have changed.'

'Evidently.'

He didn't have time for this. Orlando felt what little patience he'd had march out of the door.

Pushing back his chair, he drew himself up to

his full height and looked down on this infuriating woman. 'Look, Isobel, I'm not here to mess about or to play games. I've only got a short time in London and I thought it would be nice to spend some of it with you. Even if it's just dinner. But I'm certainly not going to force your hand.'

Standing with his feet apart he folded his arms decisively across his chest.

'If you have other plans, or would rather not, that's fine too. Just say the word.'

'Two words, actually, Orlando.'

Orlando narrowed his eyes, something about the tortured expression clouding Isobel's face halting the pumped up pride in his chest, preventing any sharp retort from escaping. Instead he grew very still.

'Go on.'

Isobel dragged in a deep breath and he found himself willing her to just damn well come out with it. But nothing, absolutely *nothing*, could have prepared him for the words when they eventually came.

'I'm pregnant.'

CHAPTER TWO

'PREGNANT?'

Isobel watched as Orlando's face turned to stone, his features hardening, his jaw clenching.

'No.' Getting to his feet, he stared down at her, his body rigid with tension. 'You can't be.'

'It's true, Orlando.' Isobel heard her reply through the roar in her ears—flat, dull, as if spoken by somebody else.

'And I am the father?'

Pain lanced through her. Did he really know her so little that he had to ask that humiliating question?

She sat up straight, bracing herself, meeting his penetrating gaze with icy contempt. 'Yes, Orlando, you are the father. Considering you are the only person I have ever had sex with, I think we can take that as definite.'

Orlando's eyes narrowed with stunned disbelief. 'The only one? You mean…?'

'Yes, exactly that. I was a virgin, Orlando.'

Darkness twisted his handsome features. 'I didn't know.' Then, more harshly, 'Why the hell didn't you say?'

'Why would I?' Isobel replied, with a calm that

threatened to shatter like glass. 'It was irrelevant. It still is irrelevant.'

'Not to me, it isn't.' Cursing under his breath, Orlando shook his head, then raised a hand to his brow.

'And this pregnancy… You are quite sure about it?'

'Quite sure.'

She let her eyes slide to the floor, to the pair of handmade Italian shoes that were planted in front of her.

The shoes moved a couple of steps away and, raising her eyes again, Isobel saw Orlando raking a hand through his hair, his expression one of abject horror.

'The split condom?' He fired the question at her as the spinning cogs of his mind whirred to find an explanation.

Isobel gave a small nod. 'It has to be.'

She had been over it a hundred times, convinced this had to be the only answer. During one of their many mad, passionate, crazy lovemaking sessions on the island of Jacamar she had heard Orlando curse, then reach out for another condom before pulling her back into his arms. She remembered the raw panting of his breath, the pounding of his heart beneath his ribcage as he straddled her once more, intent on finishing where he had left off, taking them both soaring to the heights of ecstasy they'd so badly craved.

As she had fallen asleep in his arms, sweat-sealed and sated, her body still shuddering with the aftershocks of pleasure, it had never occurred to her that the course of her life was about to change for ever.

Cursing again in his native tongue, Orlando turned on his heel, striding over to the wall of windows, where he braced his hands against the glass, resting his forehead between them. Isobel stared at the stark outline of his rear view, his stiffly held posture radiating tension.

'How long have you known?' He spoke the words over his shoulder.

'I just did the test this morning.'

Orlando spun around. 'So you haven't had it confirmed by a doctor?'

'I don't need to, Orlando.' Isobel knew she had to extinguish the look of hope in his eyes. 'These tests are extremely accurate. And, besides, I can already feel the changes in my body. I've had my suspicions for a couple of weeks, but I wanted to be absolutely sure before I told you.'

Moving away from the window, Orlando came to sit down again, pulling up his chair so that he was positioned directly opposite Isobel, close enough for his knees to brush hers. Isobel crossed her legs tightly, pulled at the hem of her skirt.

'Then we must figure out how we are going to proceed.' Running his hand over his jaw, Orlando cupped his chin, his eyes narrowing with concentration as they searched hers.

How we are going to proceed. The words made Isobel's skin prickle with alarm as she watched his wall of self-control slide back into place. Because she knew the kind of man Orlando was: powerful, ruthless. One who liked to make all the decisions, to bend others to his will. Who even now looked as if he was about to take command, address the problem of this pregnancy with cool detachment and deal with it as he saw fit.

Well, Isobel would never let that happen. She sure as hell wasn't going to have him ruling her life, calling the shots. She had done the right thing by telling him she was carrying his child, but as far as she was concerned that was it. From now on the responsibility and the decisions were all hers. She needed to make that very clear.

Leaning forward, Orlando rested his splayed hands on his thighs, his dark gaze holding hers with brooding intensity. Isobel could see his mind racing as he tried to come to terms with this information, tried to shape it into some form he could control. He was so close now she could feel the air move with each steady breath, catch the faint scent of his cologne, see the amber flecks in his eyes.

She took in a breath to try and steady the pounding of her heart. This was what Orlando did to her. He messed with her head, made her feel things she didn't want to feel. She was still trying to fight off the effects of that earlier kiss, the burning ache that had spread through her body and continued to pulse low down in her abdomen. He shouldn't have done that—it wasn't fair...he had broken the rules. Because they both knew that what had happened on Jacamar—that crazy, heady cocktail of wild abandonment and mind-blowing sex—had to stay on Jacamar.

As he had pulled away from their final hug the message in Orlando's eyes had been loud and clear. *That was great.* Emphasis on the *was*. And Isobel had played along, knowing it was the only way, ignoring the hard knot in her throat, covering up the wobble of her chin until she had been chugging away from the sunshine island with the wind in her face and horizontal tears leaking from her eyes.

Because she had known then, as she knew now, that she was going to have to fight against her feelings for Orlando with all her might. Losing her heart to this magnetic, masterful man would mean nothing but misery, that was a certainty.

Over the past couple of weeks—from the first creeping realisation that her period was late to the hideous certainty that she was pregnant—she had given serious thought to keeping the news to herself. That way she just might be able to protect her heart and control her own destiny. If Orlando didn't know about the child she would be free to raise it as she liked. Financially it would be a struggle, but she could do it. It wasn't as if she wanted anything from *him*. She wouldn't be hounding him for maintenance. And she most certainly didn't expect him to marry her.

But, tempting though it was to try and keep Orlando out of the equation, practically it would be a nightmare. And, more than that, ultimately she knew that her conscience would never let her go through with it. After all, it was a man's basic right to know that he was going to be a father.

Which was why she was seated here now, fighting off the sweeping feelings of longing with sweaty palms and a deliberately steely stare.

'It's not something you have to figure out, Orlando.' Edging back into her seat, Isobel concentrated on the job she had to do. 'I will be the one deciding how to proceed.'

'Scusi?' A muscle twitched ominously in his jaw.

'I mean I am prepared to accept full responsibility.'

'"Full responsibility"?' Dark brows drew together.

'Yes. I don't expect anything from you.' Isobel paused to take in a breath, strongly suspecting from Orlando's chilling calm that this wasn't going her way. She tried again. 'Obviously I would never stop you from seeing the child—if you want to, that is—but in terms of raising it, I want to make it clear that I expect that role to be solely down to me.'

'Do you, indeed?' Orlando's voice dropped menacingly low.

'Yes.'

'Incredibile.' Orlando pushed himself back forcibly enough for the chair to rock on its legs. 'Let me get this straight. First you tell me that I'm going to be a father, and then you hit me with the news that you intend to raise the child alone and without my support. Is that right?'

'Yes.' Isobel blinked hard but remained defiant. 'I told you because I thought you had a right to know—not because I want anything from you.'

'Very kind of you, I'm sure.' Sarcasm ripped through his voice. 'So, having been given this information, what exactly did you expect me to do with it? Say "Thanks for letting me know" and then walk away? Forget all about it?'

'If that's what you want, yes.' Isobel was determined not to buckle under the force of his contemptuous stare. 'You have that option.'

'Ha!' Orlando gave a cruel laugh. 'Believe me, I don't. And neither do *you*, come to that, no matter how much you might want it.'

'Orlando, look—'

Hearing a tap on the door, Orlando held up his hand to silence her as his PA appeared, framed prettily in the doorway.

'Not now, Astrid.'

His barked words brought a flash of surprise to Astrid's face before she quickly pulled down the mask of professionalism.

'My apologies, but I thought you would want to know that your one-thirty appointment has arrived.'

Orlando rubbed his temples. 'Yes, of course. Tell them I'll be five minutes.'

'Certainly.' Turning on her dainty heel, Astrid left the room, closing the door behind her.

'We need to talk, Isobel, but not here.' Pushing back the sleeve of his jacket, Orlando glanced at his watch. 'I have meetings all afternoon, so it will have to be this evening. I should be free by seven o'clock.'

Isobel hesitated. Part of her—a big part—wanted to decline his less-than-cordial invitation. Tell him that as far as she was concerned there was no point in spending a torturous evening together. Orlando's cold, calculating reaction to the news of her pregnancy had confirmed her worst fears. He had shown no compassion. Never once had he asked about *her*, about how she *felt*.

She had done her duty in telling him about the baby—now she just wanted to be left alone to pick up the pieces and carry on as best she could. But one glance at the determined set of Orlando's jaw, the hint of steel in his eyes, told her that that was about as likely to happen as holding back the ocean with a wall of sand.

Rising to her feet, she picked up her bag and plastered on the most neutral expression she could muster. 'Very well, if that's what you want. I'll see you this evening. Where do you want to meet?'

'Leave your address with Astrid.' Giving her no chance to disagree, Orlando stood before her, all tall, imperious command. 'I'll pick you up at seven.'

Orlando watched as Isobel hurried from the room, those provocative heels clicking accusingly on the polished wooden floor. He could hear her talking to Astrid in the outer office before finally taking her leave. Only then did he allow himself to sink down into a chair and put his head in his hands.

Pregnant.

The reality of what he had done hit him like a ton of rock, the shock firing through his veins. Isobel—a young woman he hardly knew—was pregnant with his baby. And if that wasn't bad enough she had been a virgin before he had come along and ruined her life. What sort of a brute did that make him? One just like his father, that was what—a man who had swept his teenage mother off her feet, taken what he wanted, then discarded her.

Pinching the bridge of his nose, Orlando forced himself to think. Why hadn't he *known* that Isobel was a virgin? Would it have made any difference if he had? Their brief relationship had been so sudden, so wildly all-consuming, it had knocked all the normal rules out of the park. The attraction between them had been powerful and overwhelming and impossible to resist. And it had been the same for both of them. Or so he'd thought.

Screwing up his eyes, Orlando let the image of those sultry nights play over in his mind. Yes, Isobel had wanted him—he was sure about that. He remembered them tearing each other's clothes off, remembered the look of pure sexual longing in Isobel's eyes as she had reached out to him that first time, arching her naked body against his. But now he also remembered the sharp intake of breath when he had entered her...the fat tears that had leaked from the corners of her eyes when they had finally fallen back against the pillows, gasping for breath.

At the time he had thought nothing of it—or, worse still, had maybe revelled in his potent masculinity, his ability to stir such passion in a beautiful young woman.

Now the thought of what he'd done made him

feel sick. But the deed was done—and with the most dramatic of consequences.

Somehow he had to get his head around this. *He was going to be a father.* The one thing he had always sworn would never, *ever* happen. Because Orlando had seen first-hand the brutal destruction that came with so-called family life. His own childhood was a chilling testament to that—completely chaotic from the start.

As a young boy he had been shunted from one foster family to the next, whenever his mother's fragile mental health had left her unable to cope or plunged her into a depression so black that Orlando had been deemed at risk of neglect. He had been twelve years old when she had died, unable to care for herself any better than she had her precious, skinny, vulnerable son.

Too old to be adopted, and too difficult, challenging and downright angry with the world to be suitable for short-term fostering any more, Orlando had been placed in a children's home. And that forbidding, prison-like building had been his home for more than four years.

It had been during his last few months there that he had made the disastrous decision to track down his father—the man who had had a brief affair with his mother, then abandoned her before he was born. The man who had triggered the mental health issues that had eventually led to his mother's death. The man who had very nearly destroyed Orlando too.

But all that had been a long time ago—almost half a lifetime, in fact. At just seventeen years old Orlando had bought a one-way ticket to New York and left his wretched past firmly behind him. And the years since then had been good—remarkable, even—with determination, dedication and sheer hard work seeing Orlando rise rapidly from absolutely nothing to be one of the world's most successful businessmen. A massive achievement in anyone's book.

Yes, Orlando Cassano was at the top of his game. He'd got his life exactly where he wanted it. *Or so he'd thought.*

Now not only had his past come back to haunt him, but his future was being catapulted into the unknown. He was going to have a child. He had no idea exactly what that would mean, but he did know that he would be there for his son or daughter—come what may, whatever it took. No way would he replicate the despicable behaviour of his own father.

And that meant the course of his life was about to change for ever.

'I'll be right down.'

Replacing the intercom receiver, Isobel reached for her coat and slung it over her arm. After checking her reflection in the mirror she hurried out, locking the door behind her before running down the several flights of stairs. She didn't want to give Orlando the chance to invite himself up.

Not that she was ashamed of her flat—far from it. It might be tiny, but the rent was reasonable and it was nice and central—only a few stops on the underground to the headquarters of Spicer Shoes. However, it was hardly on a par with the sort of grandeur that Orlando Cassano was accustomed to.

He was studying the view when Isobel joined him, taking in the car park, the bike racks and the group of youths sitting on the wall that housed the dustbins. Her dash down the stairs had left her out of breath, and Orlando turned to look at her, coolly objective.

Isobel fought to suppress the familiar lurch in her stomach at the sight of him. He looked ridiculously out of place, standing there in his dark grey cashmere coat, the collar pulled up against the chilly breeze. All urbane, confident authority, he seemed the very antithesis of the crudely graffitied walls of this inner-city tower block.

'How long have you lived here?'

Having performed a perfunctory kiss on both cheeks, Orlando took a couple of steps back and craned his head to look up, scanning the soulless concrete facade, the uniform rows of windows.

Isobel watched his Adam's apple move beneath the smooth olive skin.

'A couple of years.' She focussed on buttoning up her coat. 'And, before you start, there is nothing wrong with it. We can't all live on Caribbean islands or in Long Island mansions.'

'Did I say that?'

'Well, no, but...'

'In that case I'll thank you not to make accusatory assumptions.' His mouth flattened into a tight line, his eyes narrowing with warning.

Isobel scowled back—this was not a good start. She knew she was being horribly prickly, but her nerves were shot to pieces, her head all over the place. Being in Orlando's company again was pure torture, and not just because of the pregnancy, nor the fact that he obviously had no intention of letting her raise the child alone, although that was bad enough. Far worse was the realisation that for these past few weeks she had been fooling herself.

Somehow, while they had been apart, Isobel had managed to convince herself that what had happened on Jacamar—the way she had fallen head over heels for Orlando—had been the result of some sort of Caribbean magic...a spell that would be easily broken when she returned to the UK.

But that theory had vanished like an icicle in a furnace the second their eyes had met in the boardroom this morning, when the attraction Isobel had felt for him had been so powerful, so immediate, it had slammed right into her chest. And that wretched kiss hadn't helped, opening her up to all sorts of forbidden desires. She could feel them now, stubbornly pumping through her body under the grey skies of London, without a coconut or a palm tree in sight.

'My car is over here.'

He hardly needed to point it out. If Orlando seemed out of place then his gleaming car looked as if it had been dropped down from another planet. Sleek, black and low, it had certainly caught the eye of the local residents, several of whom had sauntered over to inspect it, peering in through the windows and running their hands over the immaculate paintwork.

Isobel felt familiar panic creep through her veins. Not because of the circling hooded youngsters—she'd lived here long enough to know that they wouldn't bother her—but because cars, fast cars in particular, terrified her.

She had been seventeen when a horrific car crash had all but decimated her family, killing her father and leaving her mother in a wheelchair. Isobel had received only minor injuries, but the course of her life had changed for ever.

Giving up any idea of going to university, she had determined there and then that she would honour her father by taking on the family business and dedicating herself to making Spicer Shoes a success. She'd hoped the hard work would be cathartic and that a thriving business would mean security for the loyal Spicer employees *and* for her mother, whose continuing care in a residential home was eye-wateringly expensive.

More than that, she'd hoped to be able to make her mother see that the world hadn't stopped the day of the accident. That she still had her daughter—alive and well and desperate to have a loving relationship with her, desperate to make amends.

But in the seven years that had passed, even though the business was now poised on the brink of massive success, Isobel's relationship with her mother had become more strained than ever—something that weighed more heavily on her shoulders than she would even admit to herself.

And then there were the panic attacks. The crippling anxiety that Isobel still battled against whenever she sat in a car. But time and some intensive therapy had helped—plus the determination that she was going to overcome her fear. Now, dragging in a deep breath, she released it slowly, the way she had been shown, and strode with great determination to meet her nemesis.

Opening the door for her, Orlando waited as she slid in. Distracted by the car's admiring audience, he hadn't seemed to notice Isobel's fear, which was just the way she wanted it. She waited as he went round to the driver's side, her nails digging into the palms of her hands.

'What can she do?'

Outside, she could hear a conversation starting up.

'Over two hundred, technically.'

Oh, dear God. Orlando had opened his door and was standing outside it, just the lower half of his body visible to Isobel, one foot resting on the car's sill.

'Cool. You ever done that?'

'I've taken her up to one-fifty on the autobahn in Germany and she still seemed to have plenty left.'

'Wow. That's cool, man.'

The way Isobel's anxiety levels were racing, she suspected they would give it a run for its money. Reaching across, she pressed the car horn, meaning to grab Orlando's attention so that they could get going—get this ordeal over with before she lost her nerve completely. But the jarring sound made her shrink back into her seat, and as Orlando peered in she caught his puzzled look.

'You okay?'

'Fine.' She whispered the word under her breath as she double-checked the clasp of her seat belt. 'Can we just get out of here, please?'

Swinging himself inside with cat-like agility, Orlando turned the key in the ignition and the engine roared into life. As he pressed his foot on the accelerator it growled throatily. Through the wind-screen Isobel could see the look of respect on the young men's faces.

'You seem very impatient.' He glanced at her, his hands gripping the steering wheel. 'I can't see that it hurts for me to spend a bit of time with those guys.'

'You won't say that when your car is found burnt out on a piece of wasteland.'

'And you accuse *me* of prejudice?' He gave a dismissive snort.

Isobel glared at him. 'Look, I'm not saying they are bad kids, but a flashy car like this is bound to be a target for joyriders. It's like asking for trouble.'

'Ah, so it's *my* fault.'

'I didn't say that.'

'It's important not to write people off because of their backgrounds, Isobel. I was young once. I remember what it was like.'

'I wasn't suggesting we wrote them off.' How had she dug herself into this hole? 'I happen to get on fine with my neighbours. But I doubt very much that *you* have anything in common with them.'

Orlando raised his eyebrows, as if he were about to say something, then clearly changed his mind, turning his eyes back to the front. 'I'm just saying there's no harm in treating young people with respect—giving them something to aspire to rather than assuming that the trappings of success will provoke jealousy or criminality.'

Well, that was her told. His sanctimonious conceit was almost enough to goad Isobel out of her terror. *Almost*. But as the car took off with a sudden burst of speed, its tyres screeching on the tarmac as Orlando spun it around in the opposite direction, Isobel could only shriek.

'For God's sake!'

Gripping the sides of her seat, she twisted round to look out of the rear window, convinced she'd see the bodies of her neighbours scattered in their wake. Instead she could just make out grinning faces, arms raised in gestures of respect.

'What the hell do you think you're doing?'

'It's what they expect of a car like this.'

They had slowed right down now, edging into the traffic of the main road. Isobel stared at his handsome, composed profile.

'If you dangle a dream in front of someone you don't want to disappoint them.'

Sinking down into the low leather seat, she willed her racing heart to steady. This was no dream…it was a nightmare.

CHAPTER THREE

'PLEASE, SIT DOWN.'

Up on his feet, Orlando was gesturing to the chair opposite him, his impatient gaze following Isobel's every move as she joined him at their table.

Having just about survived the car journey to the restaurant, she had made straight for the restroom to repair her make-up and give her churning stomach some time to calm down. Mercifully, the clogged London traffic had given Orlando no chance to exceed the speed limit, and when his first attempts at conversation had failed he'd accepted her silence and left her to endure the journey in peace.

She'd probably been away no more than five or six minutes, but judging by the scowl on Orlando's face it was five or six minutes too long.

'I've ordered for you.'

Leaning forward with the wine bottle in his hand, Orlando went to fill Isobel's glass but she shook her head and reached for the carafe of water.

'I know the chef here. His recommendations are always excellent.'

'Right. Thank you.' It wasn't the food Isobel was worried about. It was the way Orlando was insidiously taking control.

Taking in a breath, she looked around. They were tucked in a discreet corner of a well-known and very exclusive restaurant—the sort that took bookings for twelve months in advance…or twelve minutes if you were Orlando Cassano. She'd recognised several celebrities seated at the subtly lit, polished wood tables, and ordinarily she would have loved a discreet gawp around to see who was dining with whom. But tonight her attention was on only one person—the darkly handsome man who sat opposite her now.

'So, obviously we have a lot to discuss.' Picking up his glass, Orlando swirled the dark red wine around, already coldly businesslike. 'When exactly is the baby due?'

'The beginning of December.'

'So that gives us—what? Seven months?'

Us? Since when had they become an *us*?

Isobel took a gulp of water. 'Yes. If my calculations are right, the due date is December the second.' Just saying it out loud made it somehow seem all the more bewilderingly real.

'Well, obviously we will need to get that date confirmed by a doctor.'

'This is a *baby*, Orlando, not a business deal.' Isobel heard her own acerbic reply. 'You can't threaten it with a penalty clause if it doesn't deliver on time.'

A warning gleam shone in Orlando's eyes, but

he chose not to challenge her. Clearing his throat, he continued. 'I'll make enquiries about the best obstetrician in London.'

'There's no need. I can make my own appointments, thank you.'

'Very well.' He sighed pointedly. 'In that case, let's move on to where we are going to live.'

'Live?' Isobel carefully placed her glass down on the table. 'As in together?'

'I've been thinking maybe New York would be the most practical. I have a large apartment there, and—'

'Wait a minute, Orlando. I can't move to *New York*!' Isobel gasped with panic. 'My home, my business—everything is here in London.'

'Spicer Shoes is a global company now, Isobel. Isn't that what you've been striving for? With the new flagship store on Fifth Avenue opening soon it wouldn't hurt for you to be seen to be spending some time in the US—charity galas, opening nights…that sort of thing. All good for business.' He paused, meeting her heated gaze with measured calmness. 'As for your home—what are you suggesting? That I move into your apartment? I suspect it would be a little crowded for the three of us.'

Isobel scowled. The idea of him moving into her flat was farcical, as well he knew.

She squared her shoulders. 'I don't remember agreeing to us living together at all.'

'We are both going to have to make sacrifices, Isobel.' Orlando pinned her with his gaze. 'That's the fact of the matter.'

Sacrifices. Was that how he saw this? Was that how he viewed their baby?

Because that wasn't how Isobel felt. She already loved this growing life inside her—already knew that she would do anything to protect it, to provide for it, to keep it safe. That wasn't sacrifice—that was love. But it wasn't the same for Orlando— how could it be? He had no emotional attachment to this baby. To him it was just a millstone around his neck, a huge encumbrance that he felt compelled to deal with.

With a spark of hope, Isobel decided to give it one more try—to make him realise that he could walk away if he wanted to, leave her to it. She could cope. In fact she would trade the tumult of living with him for the hollow calmness of raising the child alone a thousand times over.

'I meant what I said earlier, Orlando,' she started. 'I am prepared to raise the child alone, to take full responsibility. There is no need for you to make any sacrifices for this baby.'

'Let me make something clear, Isobel.' Orlando's voice dipped dangerously low. 'I intend to meet my responsibilities, and that will inevitably involve sacrifices. But I will make them willingly and wholeheartedly. It's the only way. I assume you feel the same?'

'Well, yes, obviously.' It was all very well, him coming over all noble, but he expected her to give up her life in London and fly halfway across the world to share a life with him that he freely admitted would only be for the sake of their child.

Deep down, Isobel knew that was what hurt most of all. And deep down was where that particular misery was going to have to stay. Because she had more than enough to worry about right now.

'I know that having a baby will radically alter my lifestyle, but not to the extent that I have to leave England and move to another continent.'

'Do you have a better idea?'

Isobel sucked in a breath, all too aware that Orlando was poised, ready to pounce. Still, she had to try. 'I don't see why you can't successfully be a part of the child's life even if we live in different places.'

There was a telling pause. Orlando's eyes were holding hers with an icy sharpness that lowered the temperature by several degrees. Dimly Isobel registered the burble of voices, the throaty laugh of a woman on the table behind them, the ominous drum of Orlando's fingers on the table.

'I don't want to be "a part of the child's life", Isobel.' When finally he spoke his voice was low, but full of intent. 'I want to be a *father*.'

The weighting of the word left no room for mis-understanding.

Squaring his shoulders, he gave Isobel the full force of his gaze, those deliciously dark, bitter chocolate eyes piercing her with almost painful intensity.

'And I mean a father from the get-go—starting now. I will be supporting it financially, emotionally, and any other way that is necessary. I will be involved in all decisions regarding every aspect of its life until it reaches adulthood, and after that too—whenever he or she wishes it or I deem it to be required. I am going to be one hundred per cent committed to our child. Do I make myself clear?'

Isobel swallowed.

'And one more thing.' He set his jaw determinedly. 'We will need to get married.'

Orlando coldly watched the look of panic sweep over Isobel's face, The irony of the situation was striking a heavy blow to his pride. Never had he expected his marriage proposal to be met with such a reaction. But then never had he expected to make one.

Life for him was all about working hard and taking his pleasures when and where he chose—usually in the form of beautiful women and always, *always* on his terms. Marriage was for mugs. And as for children... Based on his own upbringing, they brought nothing but misery and heartache.

But circumstances had changed dramatically and the unimaginable had happened. Now he was determined to make Isobel his wife, no matter how distasteful she might find it. Because no way was he going to have his child growing up illegitimate, as he had. No way was he going to follow the pattern of his father in any shape or form.

In the few hours he'd had to get used to the idea of Isobel's pregnancy, shock had turned to discipline as adrenaline had kicked in, telling him to take charge, control the situation, do what he did best. Now he was intent on working out the practicalities, finding the best way to make a stable home for this child. Because that was how Orlando worked—logically, methodically, with a cool head and a razor-sharp brain that defined and solved problems.

It was a winning combination that had served him well in business, kept him ahead of the game, made him the hugely successful man he was today.

But logic couldn't account for the tightening in his chest when he looked at Isobel now. Or why her expression—*sheer horror* just about summed it up—twisted at something inside him. If he had asked her to jump off a cliff she couldn't have looked more aghast. He had no idea why that look bothered him—it wasn't as if he was even surprised.

'Married?' Finally finding her voice, Isobel used

it with chilling authority. 'No, I'm sorry. I can't commit to that.'

Orlando felt the blood start to pulse in his veins. 'I'm afraid you are going to have to.'

'I don't *have* to do anything, Orlando.'

Isobel's stark words pulled him up short, and as the waiter arrived with their food Orlando was forced to accept that she was right. Right now, Isobel held all the cards. There was absolutely nothing to stop her from digging in those sexy heels and refusing point-blank to agree to any of his demands. Or, worse still, striding off in them and leaving him with nothing but a foul temper and a pending paternity case.

He watched from beneath lowered lashes as she looked at the food being set before her, politely thanking the waiter. If he wasn't careful he was going to blow this. His every instinct was telling him that he *had* to win control of this situation, of Isobel—of his whole life, goddammit. Because at the moment he was still in free fall, with no idea of where he might land.

A huge surge of emotion was telling him to get this sorted *right now*. He would have frog-marched Isobel to a register office there and then if he'd thought he could get away with it. But he knew he had to rein in his domineering attitude before it spooked Isobel completely and she bolted out of his life.

He picked up his knife and fork. 'I'm sorry you find the idea so abhorrent, Isobel.' His knife sliced through a scallop with a surgeon's precision. 'But I think it's important that we establish some security for our child as soon as possible. Things can change...who knows what might happen in the future?'

'Meaning what, exactly?'

'Meaning you might meet someone else—find a lovely roses-round-the-door family life that I would have no part in.'

'No, that wouldn't happen.'

'It's possible.'

'So what are you saying? We have to marry in order for you to have legal rights over the child?'

'That is one of the reasons.'

'In that case let me give you my word right now. I would never dispute the child's parentage nor deny you access.'

'Not good enough, I'm afraid.'

'Well, then, have a legal document drawn up. I'll sign whatever you like to say that I will never keep you from your child.'

'That's what I intend to do.' Orlando's closed, commanding features held her gaze. 'It's called a marriage certificate.'

They stared at each other across the table. A pulse throbbed at the base of Orlando's throat. He was only just hanging on—to his authority and to his temper.

It didn't help that Isobel's every movement seemed to be hot-wired to his libido, firing his lust in a way he could barely keep under control. He could feel it racing through him as he watched her eating now. There was something incredibly sexy about the nip of her teeth, the slight sheen of oil on her pink lips.

Forcing himself to release some of the tension, to allow his features to soften, Orlando tried a different tack. 'Look, Isobel, there is still a stigma attached to growing up illegitimate—I should know…it happened to me. I don't want that burden for our child. I won't allow it.'

He watched Isobel's expression change, her eyes soften at this crumb of a confession he had tossed her. Which, perversely, made him regret telling her. Because he didn't want to achieve his aim through weakness. Orlando Cassano got what he wanted through strength, intelligence—cunning, even. Those were the attributes he felt comfortable with—the attributes that had taken him from runaway street urchin to billionaire businessman in the space of a decade.

But his success was of no interest to Isobel. Orlando already knew that much. Aside from funding her precious business, his wealth and fortune meant nothing. No amount of money was going to impress her, and clearly chest-beating was not the way to get her to agree to his terms. But maybe shedding a chink of light on his past life would do it. If that was what it took, he would go there. But a chink was all she was getting…

'Your parents weren't married, then?' Isobel put down her knife and fork.

'No.'

'Did they live together? As a couple, I mean?'

'I was the product of a sordid affair. My father was married to someone else at the time, and when he found out my mother was pregnant he disowned her. There was a protracted paternity case, because my mother was determined that I should bear the Cassano name. I wish to God she hadn't bothered.'

Reaching for her glass of water, Isobel raised it to her lips, regarding him with interest. 'So your father was eventually forced to acknowledge you?'

'Yeah.' Orlando felt his jaw clench. 'But that was as far as it went.'

If he'd had his way this would have been the end of the conversation, but with Isobel's green gaze still searching his he knew he was going to have to give her more.

'I looked him up when I turned seventeen. We had a brief relationship. It didn't work out.'

That was the understatement of the millennium. Deciding to acquaint himself with his father had been the single worst decision of his life.

Poised on the brink of manhood, the seventeen-year-old Orlando had decided he wanted to see this man for himself—to look him in the eye even if was just to let him know exactly how contemptible Orlando thought he was.

But it hadn't turned out like that. Handsome and charismatic, Carlo Cassano hadn't been the man Orlando had been expecting at all—and neither had he expected the welcome he'd received, the open-armed enthusiasm of Carlo Cassano for his long-lost son. His father had offered him a glimpse of a world of glamour and wealth that bore no resemblance to the austerity of the children's home or the misery of his early childhood with his mother. As Marchese di Trevente he lived a life of money and power, fast cars and glamorous women.

And Orlando had been hooked.

Choosing to ignore everything his mother had told him over the years—including the hysterical rants and wailing sobs that had accompanied the name Carlo Cassano every time it had been mentioned—he had decided *this* was the life he wanted. So when his father had offered him a home, told him he should come and work for him, Orlando had jumped at the chance. Little knowing that his mother's bitterly miserable opinion of him had barely scratched the surface.

For in truth his father had been far more immoral, far more depraved than even she had known, and Orlando's brief association with him had resulted in the worst possible tragedy—the death of a young woman… Sophia, Orlando's girlfriend and first love. Orlando would never, ever forgive his father for what had happened. And, what was more, he would never forgive himself.

'And now?' Isobel was persisting with her needling questions. 'Do you know where he is?'

'I do.' His voice sounded harsh and he cursed it for betraying him. 'Buried in the family plot on the Trevente estate.

'I'm sorry.'

'Well, *I'm* not.' He could rot in hell as far as Orlando was concerned.

'Trevente…' Isobel narrowed her eyes thoughtfully. 'Isn't that in the Le Marche region of Italy?'

'Correct.'

A dawning realisation slowly spread across her beautiful face. 'So you grew up in Le Marche? That's why you suggested siting the Spicer Shoes factory there? Why you were able to locate the premises so quickly?'

'I have contacts all over the world.' Orlando returned to his food. 'Le Marche is well known for producing luxury leather goods. It was the logical solution.'

'Logical… Yes, of course.'

Her smug remark stuck in his craw, but Orlando

refused to let her see it. 'Perhaps now you can see why we need to marry. Our child needs the stability of legitimacy and, frankly, so do I.'

There—he had said his piece and that was all she was getting. He looked across the table to see that Isobel had lowered her eyes to her barely touched plate of seafood, her slender fingers fiddling with a lock of chestnut hair. She appeared poised, so elegant, with that graceful style she had, but closer inspection revealed the effort involved in holding that spine so straight, the fact that her shoulders were hitched a bit too high.

'It is a huge commitment, Orlando.'

'I know that.'

Finally he could feel her weakening. If his confession had cost him a sliver of pride, he could see that Isobel was hanging on to hers for dear life.

He deliberately softened his voice. 'But then so is having child.'

'If I do agree to marry you—and it is *if*, Orlando—you will have to respect my one condition.'

'Go ahead.'

'I want us to wait until after the baby is born.'

Steepling his hands under his chin, Orlando gazed at Isobel's determined face, weighing up his options.

'Okay.'

He would accept her decision. For now, at least, that would have to do.

* * *

'You have a visitor.'

Daisy, a young intern working for Spicer Shoes, came through from the workshop and stuck her head around the door of Isobel's office. From seeing her flushed cheeks and the exaggerated widening of her eyes Isobel already knew who the visitor was. Orlando Cassano had that kind of effect on women.

Isobel massaged her temples. She really was in no mood this morning to take any more of Orlando's bullying. The torturous meal last night had been more than enough, thank you. That meal during which…oh, yes…she had somehow found herself agreeing to marry him.

Pleading a headache had cut short the evening, and Isobel had found herself travelling home in the back of a taxi, trying to put the pieces of her life back together. If she had thought being pregnant was enough of a shock—with the worry and responsibility, the dramatic changes it would mean to her life—she now found herself caught up in the giddying, controlling world of Orlando Cassano. And it was a frighteningly dangerous place to be. For her freedom, her sanity, and most of all for her virgin heart.

For Isobel's heart had never been touched by desire before. Broken by her father's death, yes. Tortured by her fractured relationship with her mother, definitely. But love…? That was something that happened to other people and she had no use for it.

The fateful car accident had seen to that. Isobel had immediately erected a wall of self-imposed emotional isolation as punishment for what had happened and insurance against any happy-ever-after for her. After all, hadn't her mother spelled out quite clearly that the accident had not only taken away her husband but also ruined her life? Isobel had been responsible for the accident; therefore she didn't deserve happiness. It was as simple as that. So she would make sure it never crossed her path.

Not that falling in love with Orlando would ever make her happy—quite the reverse. Feeling her heart beating wildly inside her chest now, she knew that she was going to have to protect it at all costs. But a fretful night of tossing and turning had led to the creeping realisation that maybe Orlando was right about one thing. The baby was the most important thing here. Maybe it *would* be for the best for him or her to have legally married parents.

Isobel had never really thought about the stigma of illegitimacy before, having been raised by two parents in a relationship of marriage—albeit a marriage made up of more quarrels than hugs. Isobel's memories were of fights, of hiding her head under her pillow to block out screaming rows, and of vowing that she would never marry and subject herself to such torment.

Her mother's memories, however, were somewhat different. Since the accident that had so tragically taken her husband away from her, Isobel's mother had elevated her father to a level of sainthood and their marriage to the most perfect relationship that had ever been. Something that she liked to remind Isobel of whenever she visited, and which compounded Isobel's guilt like a pile driver pounding into the subsoil of her consciousness.

But illegitimacy had obviously affected Orlando, despite the emotionless way he had described it to her. And that glimpse of his vulnerability had gone straight to her heart—no doubt as he had meant it to. It had all been calculated to ensure that he got his own way. But at least she had managed to delay any idea of a wedding until after the baby was born. That had been her one small victory. And it had given her some breathing space, if nothing else.

However, today had brought another problem—in the form of a large delivery of samples from the first production line at the new factory in Le Marche. Excitement had turned to dismay as Isobel had pulled them from their boxes. The stitching was too big, the colours the wrong shade, the finish poor. Now the offending articles were scattered across her desk in a jumble of packaging and tissue paper and general frustration.

'I don't want to see anyone right now, Daisy.' Isobel tucked her hair behind her ears. 'Please say that I am busy.'

'I can see that.' Towering over Daisy's shoulder, Orlando's honed physique now filled the doorway. 'What is this? Shoe rage?'

Daisy's annoying giggle only darkened Isobel's mood—especially as she had now stepped aside to let Orlando enter. Suddenly the room seemed far too small, the ceiling too low, the clutter that was everywhere closing in on them.

Giving him the briefest of glances, Isobel turned back to her desk to wait for the spike in her heart rate to steady. 'This isn't a good time, Orlando.'

Totally ignoring her, Orlando moved in closer, looking down at the array of shoes. 'Samples from the new factory?'

'Yes, and they are dreadful.' Rummaging around, Isobel found the worst culprit and held it aloft by its spiky heel, pointing it at Orlando like a weapon. 'I can't accept this sort of quality. Quite apart from the colour being totally wrong, look at this.' She held the ankle strap between her fingers. 'The holes aren't even lined up properly.'

But as Orlando bent over her Isobel immediately regretted her invitation. Suddenly he was way too close, and she was painfully aware of the tightness in her chest, of her breasts swelling beneath her lacy cotton blouse.

'Let me see.' Rescuing the shoe from her hand, Orlando squinted at the holes on the strap before turning to the star-struck Daisy, who was still staring at him as if he was some sort of god. 'Looks okay to me. What do you think... Daisy, isn't it?'

Daisy nodded.

'It doesn't matter what Daisy thinks.' Snatching back the shoe, Isobel shoved it into the nearest box and stuffed tissue paper on top of it. '*I* am the one who decides these things, and *I* am saying that this standard is simply unacceptable.'

'Well, no doubt it can be sorted out. Let's start with coffee.'

'Yes, of course.' Daisy sprang out of her trance. 'What can I get for you?'

'Espresso—thank you.'

'Isobel?'

'Nothing for me.' Her curt reply was partly down to annoyance that Orlando was taking charge—*again*—and partly a newly acquired aversion to coffee. Another pregnancy-related surprise.

Pulling out a chair, Orlando squeezed in beside her. Isobel's basement office wasn't meant for more than one person. With its wide table, positioned beneath a glass window to let in some natural light, it worked fine as a place for Isobel to work on her designs, catch up on paperwork. But it did *not* feel fine right now, with Orlando taking up far too much space, somehow managing to steal the air that she needed to fill her lungs.

'There are bound to be some teething problems with the new factory.' Picking up a jewel-studded evening sandal, he turned it over in his hand before it was snatched back by Isobel. 'It's only to be expected.'

'I know that.' The shoes were now being swept from the table into the large cardboard box they had arrived in. 'But this is more than teething problems—this is a disaster.'

'Not a disaster. You need to remember that these shoes are for the ready-to-wear collection. You're not going to get the same quality of manufacture from the factory as you do from your guys here in the workshop.' He jerked his head towards the glass-panelled door. 'That sort of craftsmanship is for the couture trade only.'

'Well, thank you *so* much for pointing that out.' Isobel shot him a witheringly contemptuous look. 'But when I want your opinion of my business I will ask for it.'

If she'd hoped to put him in his place she was to be disappointed. Orlando appeared completely unmoved. And that annoyed her all the more.

'Can I ask what you are actually *doing* here?' She tried again. 'I'm sure you must have any number of business interests that require your attention more than mine.'

'I think our relationship has progressed somewhat further than business.'

There was that infuriating calmness again—swinging like a lead weight between them, knocking aside Isobel's protests and somehow giving him all the power.

Turning to the distraction of her computer, Isobel caught sight of her own anxious expression in the black screen before it came to life with a string of emails. She positioned her fingers over the keyboard, hoping she was making it quite clear that it was time for Orlando to leave. But it seemed he had other ideas.

'As it happens, I might be able to help you with the problem of these samples.'

Opening her first email, Isobel gave it her full attention. 'I doubt that very much.'

'I'm flying to Italy this afternoon. I have some business in Le Marche. I can go to the factory and speak to the supervisor about your concerns.'

'That won't be necessary.' Emails forgotten, Isobel turned to face him, a dangerous flash in her green eyes. 'When Cassano Holdings invested in Spicer Shoes it was with the understanding that I would have complete control of the day-to-day running of the business. The issue with these samples is *my* problem, not yours, and *I* will be the one to rectify it.'

'If you say so.' Leaning back in his chair, Orlando tried to stretch out his long legs under the table. But the space was too small and he ended up nudging Isobel's foot with his own.

Isobel edged away.

There was a moment of silence between them.

'Are you able to fly?'

Isobel stared at him, nonplussed. What did he mean by that? 'I'm pregnant, Orlando. I haven't developed super powers.'

Orlando bit back the hint of a smile. 'What I mean is, is there any reason for you not to accompany me to Le Marche?'

Isobel could think of a hundred reasons, but none of them were to do with her being pregnant.

'I have a private jet leaving this afternoon and I suggest you come with me—see the factory for yourself, sort out the problems face to face.'

'I couldn't possibly.' Casting around, Isobel desperately tried to come up with a plausible reason to say no. She couldn't go—not this afternoon, not just like that. *Not with him.* 'I'm afraid I have far too much to do here.'

'I'm sure something can be arranged.'

Right on cue the office door opened and a smiling Daisy appeared, bearing Orlando's espresso before her like a sacrificial offering.

'I bet Daisy could keep things ticking over here if you went away for a couple of days—couldn't you, Daisy?'

'Of course.' The smile turned into a beam of pleasure. 'No problem at all. You can trust me to make sure that everything runs smoothly.'

'That's settled, then.' Turning back to Isobel, Orlando let his gaze rake over Isobel's flustered figure. When he spoke again his voice was as dark as bitter chocolate. 'The flight is booked for four p.m. I'll meet you here at three.'

CHAPTER FOUR

WANDERING THROUGH THE narrow cobbled streets of Trevente, Isobel felt her spirits soar. She had had a good day.

Her visit to the factory had gone well. The head of production had given her a tour of the site, introducing her to the technical manager, the pattern cutters and the machinists. Everyone had shown real enthusiasm and commitment and had soon understood the sort of quality and attention to detail that Isobel expected. Suddenly she felt excited about her business again. *This* was what she had been working towards ever since the name Spicer Shoes had so dramatically hit the headlines.

The madness had kicked off three months ago, when an A-list actress being interviewed on prime-time television had taken offence at one of the questions being asked of her. Slipping off her shoe, she had looked as if she was going to chuck it at her interviewer, before changing her mind and speaking the now famous phrase.

'You know what? I'm not going to risk damaging my Spicer shoe on you. No man is worth that.'

Suddenly everyone had been talking about Spicer Shoes, social media had gone crazy, and before Isobel had known it she'd been swamped with an avalanche of orders from the rich and famous the world over.

It had meant a huge change for the small business. Started over fifty years ago by her grandfather, Spicer Shoes had always catered for an exclusive but relatively modest clientele. Indeed, since Isobel had been in charge there had been several times when money had been so tight she'd worried about finding the wages for her team of twelve master shoemakers employed in the workshop.

That had all changed overnight. Even though Isobel had known this massive boost of publicity would bring challenges of its own—not least a serious cash-flow problem—it had been far too good an opportunity to pass up, and she had immediately decided she was going to run with it.

And run she had—straight into the arms of Orlando Cassano.

So far today Isobel had been spared his brooding company, and she was thankful for that. Because if Orlando's mood had been brisk and businesslike when they were in London, being on Italian soil had seen it nosedive into sullenness.

It had been late last night when they had arrived at their hotel—a stunning converted monastery perched on the edge of a cliff. With huge vaulted stone ceilings and glass floors, and startlingly modern furniture, it was obviously the work of a creative genius—and *very* Orlando Cassano. They had been shown to their suite of rooms and Isobel had been relieved to see that the enormous space meant she would finally be able to get away from the man whose close proximity on the journey, together with the bleak mood that surrounded him, had done nothing to make her feel any less stressed.

Quickly choosing one of the two bedrooms, she had shut herself away, too tired to try and analyse why he was being so taciturn but assuming it was because of her and the baby and the realisation that he was well and truly trapped. Which was down to him. After all, hadn't she tried to offer him a no-strings, get-out deal?

This morning his mood had been blacker than ever. Rapping on her bedroom door, he had awoken her from a deep sleep, seen her scrabbling to pull the bedcovers over her even though she'd been wearing her favourite old pyjamas—chosen not just for their comfort value but as a practical reminder that this trip was going to be *purely* business. He had stood silhouetted in the doorway, the brilliant sunshine outlining his towering figure with a golden line of brightness, and informed her that he was leaving to attend to the mysterious business he had here in Italy. He'd told her a driver would be at her disposal to take her to the factory, and that he would meet her this evening in Trevente. And with that he had closed the door and been gone.

Trevente had turned out to be nothing short of shoe heaven. A medieval town, high on the hills of the Le Marche district of Italy, it was home to an astonishing array of different kinds of shoe shops. There were old-fashioned cobblers and bootmakers, with their workshops tucked behind shops not much bigger than a street kiosk, their wares reverentially displayed in the small shop windows like the treasures they were. Then there were the more prestigious establishments—big, famous names, with lavish window displays that took your breath away with their artistry and inventiveness.

The whole town felt like a celebration of the art of beautiful footwear and Isobel loved it—especially on this beautiful May evening, with the air filled with the scent of orange blossom and the narrow streets still busy with shoppers and diners despite the relatively late hour. It was impossible not to feel uplifted.

She was staring with rapt attention at a particularly beautiful display of shoes suspended on wires from the ceiling when she sensed she was no longer alone.

'Here you are.'

The low, distinctly surly voice spun her head around and she found herself facing the broad expanse of a muscled chest beneath an open black leather jacket.

'We had a dinner date, remember?' Orlando's scowl narrowed his eyes.

Isobel pushed back her sleeve and glanced at her watch. *Oops.* She was supposed to have met him in a local trattoria half an hour ago. 'I'm sorry. I lost track of time. This place is so amazing.'

She risked a smile, then wished she hadn't when it was met with a wall of hostility.

'Considerably less amazing when you are hungry.' Placing the flat of his hand against the small of her back, Orlando steered her away from the shop window, then linked his arm through hers—to move her in the direction he wanted her to go rather than as any display of companionship. 'The trattoria is this way.'

Hurrying to keep up with him, Isobel found herself being navigated through a series of empty back streets so narrow that she could almost stretch out and touch the tall buildings on either side. Above them fancy iron balconies were festooned with washing, and colourful plants spilled out of recycled oil containers.

All this Isobel registered at the impatient pace of her companion, who showed no sign of slowing down or making any sort of conversation. Slanting a glance at him revealed a jaw set with grim determination, and the muted orange street light glancing off harsh cheekbones, shadowing his deep-set eyes.

He was overreacting, surely? Okay, she was late. But it wasn't that big a crime—no one had died.

Tugging her arm from his grip, she finally managed to halt his march. 'Can we slow down, please?' Tossing back her head, she placed her hands squarely on her hips in true Italian *mamma* style. 'You are going too fast for me.'

Orlando's intense gaze raked over her as they stood in the dusky shadows of an alleyway. Maybe stopping hadn't been such a good idea. Suddenly her breathing felt too shallow, and her chest was rising and falling too fast.

'It's these boots.' Leaning back against the wall, she lifted her leg to inspect a heel and escape his stare. 'They weren't designed to take cobbles at high speed.'

'Evidently.' He was closer now—so close that she could feel the heat emanating from him as he looked down at her foot, feel the whisper of his breath against her hair. 'What sort of crazy design are these anyway?'

Isobel waited to draw in a sensible breath before returning her leg to the ground and tipping her face to meet his. 'They are from my new collection.' Shoes she could talk about—a nice safe topic of conversation. 'A sort of cross between a slave sandal and a boot.' As Orlando's lowered gaze raked over her open-toed footwear, over the long leather thongs that laced up the front, the topic started to feel a whole lot less safe. 'I think they will prove to be popular.'

'I don't doubt it.'

Something about Orlando's low growl set her pulse racing off at a gallop—especially when it was matched with the unmistakably male gleam in his eyes. Swallowing hard, she ordered herself to get a grip.

'However—' she gave a small cough '—had I known we would be using these backstreets as a race track I would have worn my trainers.'

'I'm glad you didn't.'

At the sound of an approaching scooter Orlando came still closer, placing the flat of his palms on the wall on either side of her head. With every nerve ending in Isobel's body singing with anticipation, she had to stifle an involuntary gasp.

'I happen to like your boots very much.'

Argh, now he was being nice to her. And that, combined with his lethal nearness, was more than Isobel's poor overloaded senses could take.

The scooter put-putted past, giving them a cheery toot as it did so. But still Orlando didn't move away, looking down on her, his breath warm on her face. 'In fact I think your designs are brilliant.'

'Thank you.' Miraculously her voice seemed to be operating normally, even if the rest of her had gone into free fall.

For a long moment Orlando stared at her, the eye contact between them producing clenching waves that pulsed low in her abdomen. She felt her lips parting in unconscious invitation as she waited, her breath high in her throat. Slowly Orlando's head lowered until his mouth was no more than a whisper away from hers. The world began to do a giddy spin.

'Which is one of the reasons I agreed to invest in Spicer Shoes.'

Right, of course it was. A little voice inside her head was clamouring to find out what the other reasons might be, but before Isobel had a chance to go there Orlando had pushed himself away from the wall and with one last, punishing stare had moved away, leaving Isobel nakedly exposed.

'Now, is there any chance we might actually make it to this restaurant?'

Lusardi's was small and cosy, with a heavenly aroma of garlic and onions that made her mouth water as soon as they entered. With candles on the basic wooden tables, it had an intimate charm that Isobel immediately loved. The trattoria was full of noisy families—several generations chattering and laughing: rotund Italian men with their napkins tucked under their chin, tiny tots wielding full-sized cutlery as they put food into their small mouths.

The table that Orlando and Isobel were shown to was squashed into a small space, and the neighbouring diners obligingly pulled in their chairs and shifted their tables to give them a bit more room. Even so, Isobel was acutely aware of Orlando's long legs brushing against hers as they tried to find some room under the table. She could sense the heat of his body in the confined space.

But the service was fast and efficient, and very soon they were tucking into delicious plates of *fritto misto*, stuffed olives and the most delectable truffle lasagne that Isobel could ever have imagined. She ate hungrily, realising she had hardly eaten anything all day, really enjoying the food. But she couldn't say the same for the company.

Opposite her, Orlando had devoured his meal with a determined concentration that Isobel had decided she wasn't even going to try to interrupt. Her brief attempts at conversation had been scythed down in favour of the food in front of him, so she had given up and left him to it. But that didn't stop her being so aware of his presence that her body seemed to vibrate with it, making her fidget in her seat, cross and uncross her legs beneath the cramped table, pull at the neckline of her sleeveless dress in an attempt to cool herself down.

Raising a forkful of pasta to her mouth, she finally allowed her eyes to settle on the lowered dark head of the man opposite. It was impossible not to be drawn in by this hypnotic, hauntingly charismatic man. In one way he seemed very much at home here—speaking in rapid Italian to the waiter, exuding his own particular autocratic air. But there was something that Isobel couldn't quite put her finger on. A silent unease that hovered around him like a dark cloud…

Raising his head from his meal, Orlando was immediately trapped by the sea-green gaze of his companion. Wide eyes were staring at him—watchful, wary, beautiful.

He knew his behaviour was puzzling Isobel, but right now he didn't seem to have his usual reserves of good manners and he couldn't do anything about it. His urbane charm had deserted him in favour of something much darker, more primal—something he couldn't control.

His visit to the family solicitor that morning had been every bit as bad as he had expected. The hope in the old man's eyes as he had formally unrolled the parchment deeds for Orlando's signature had very soon been extinguished. After solemnly shaking Orlando's hand, and addressing him by his new title—Marchese di Trevente—he had asked him about his plans for the Trevente estate. His optimism that Orlando would be the man to rescue the failing, run-down estate had been quite unmissable. *And misplaced.* As Orlando had wasted no time in telling him.

On hearing that he intended to put the whole place up for sale immediately, the solicitor had simply returned the heavy wooden seal to its velvet box, then looked down at the hardening wax next to Orlando's signature with a look of deep regret.

It was only afterwards that Orlando had realised that by trying so hard to distance himself from his father, to make it clear that he was his son in name only, and that he wanted nothing to do with the title *or* the Trevente estate, he had actually displayed the sort of boorish behaviour that his father had been well known for. And that had done nothing to improve his mood.

And neither did sitting in this cramped restaurant with Isobel. Bringing her here had been a mistake. They could have gone for a meal anywhere—back to their hotel, with its cool air-conditioning and its Michelin-starred chef. Instead he had chosen this steamy, stuffy, frankly sweaty little trattoria. And why? Because he'd known that Isobel would like it here, that was why. A fact borne out by the way she was hungrily wolfing down her meal.

He had wanted to show her Trevente too—something that had surprised him, considering his own overwhelming urge to get the hell out of the place and never come back. But he'd known she would love it and the sparkle in her eyes when he had caught her gazing at the shoes in that shop window had told him he'd been right about that too.

Even if he'd felt a ridiculous pang of jealousy because she didn't look at him that way.

Placing his knife and fork together, he told himself to focus on the practicalities of the situation he found himself in. Which meant getting shot of his unwanted inheritance and figuring out the best way forward with Isobel and the baby. What he *shouldn't* be doing was allowing himself to wallow in this darkly introspective mood.

He needed to take control. But for some reason being around Isobel Spicer was making that spectacularly difficult—in fact everything about her was pulling him apart. From the sassy sway of her slender figure when she walked, to the velvet pout of her lips as she ate, even the obstinate tilt of her chin when she insisted on challenging him turned him on.

Not to mention the flashing green eyes that were focussed on him now…

Dio. He could have taken her just now, in that dark alley. Pressed her up against the wall, pushed up her short dress with hands that would have trembled with need until he found her panties and the sweet pleasure that lay beneath. And what sort of grubby behaviour would *that* have been for a thirty-four-year-old man who prided himself on his masterly control?

He blamed it on those boots. As he watched Isobel scan the dessert menu he thought back to the way the thick curtain of her hair had fallen across her face as she had held her heel in her hand, the balletic angle of her raised leg making all sorts of improper thoughts race through his mind. The thought of undoing those leather thongs still taunted him now, even though they were safely hidden under the table.

'So.' Clearing his throat, he made a conscious effort to push aside his absurd adolescent fantasies. 'How did it go at the factory today?'

'Good...yes.' She looked at him over the top of the laminated menu. 'It's very impressive—all those brand-new machines and the machinists already in place. I can't believe how quickly it has been set up.'

'Several factories have gone under since the recession, and unemployment is high in this region—plenty of skilled machinists looking for work.' Orlando paused while the waiter took Isobel's order for chocolate soufflé, declining his invitation to join her with a raised hand. 'I knew this area would be an ideal site for the Spicer factory.'

'You were right. It was great to see for myself where your investment is being spent. And everyone seemed very enthusiastic and committed.'

'So they should be. This is the start of a very productive relationship that means food on the table for these people, security for their families—and healthy bonuses too, if all goes well and the business takes off as predicted.'

'Let's hope so.' Isobel shot him a tender smile that threatened to undo him. A pulse throbbed at the base of her slender neck, giving away just how much this business meant to her.

'And the quality control you were so worried about?' Forcing himself to concentrate on business, he continued. 'Did you manage to resolve that?'

'Yes, I think so.' She levelled dancing green eyes at him. 'I have to confess I may have overreacted a bit when I first saw the samples.'

Orlando thought back to yesterday morning in her office, to the discarded pile of shoes and the upturned boxes that had been strewn across her desk. To the mood she had been in as she had tossed them around—the flush of her cheeks, her eyes glittering dangerously.

'Oh, I don't know... The spacing of the holes on that strap... Enough to tip *anyone* over the edge, I would have thought.'

There was a pause as Isobel stared at him, obviously struggling to believe that he was teasing her, that he was actually being light-hearted. *When had he turned into such a grouch?* But as her full lips slowly curved into a smile that lit up her face and his blood rushed south with dizzying speed he remembered just why he had to be so careful around her.

'Okay, point taken!' As the waiter set her dessert before her Isobel dug in her spoon and took a mouthful, closing her eyes with pleasure. 'Mmm... This is delicious.' Reloading her spoon, she held it towards him. 'Would you like to try some?'

'Um...no—*no grazie*.' Orlando dragged his eyes away, folding his arms firmly across his chest.

'So...' Licking the chocolate from her lips, Isobel continued. 'How was *your* day? You haven't told me yet what business has brought you to Trevente.'

Orlando hesitated. No, he hadn't, had he? And if he had his way he wouldn't. But something about the way Isobel was looking at him, those wide eyes searching his face for clues, weakened his resolve. What did it matter if he told her? It was done now.

'I came here to sign for my inheritance.'

'Really?' Isobel replaced her spoon on its saucer. 'What inheritance is that?'

Ah, that had piqued her interest, hadn't it? He'd got her attention now. Orlando dragged in a breath.

'Castello Trevente...the Trevente estate.' He paused, almost enjoying the look of astonishment on Isobel's face. 'Oh, and the title that goes with it—Marchese di Trevente.'

'No!' Isobel touched her napkin to her lips. 'Are you telling me that you are a *marquess*?'

'If that's what you call it in England—then, yes. But before you start getting the cards printed perhaps I had better tell you that I intend to renounce the title—and sell the estate and the *castello*, come to that. Assuming I can find anyone fool enough to buy it, of course.'

'Sell it? Why on earth would you do that?'

'It doesn't matter why.' Bored with the subject, Orlando turned to find the waiter. 'Are you ready to leave?'

'Not yet.' Reaching forward, Isobel covered his hand with her own, then released it again as if it had scorched her. Orlando raised his eyebrows. 'I'm just asking, Orlando. I mean, presumably this title has been in your family for generations?'

Orlando shrugged his indifference.

'Don't you have a duty to protect it? To pass it on to the next generation?'

'No, I don't. And frankly this is none of your business.' He ground out the words through a clenched jaw. Opening his wallet, he threw a bunch of euro notes down on to the table. 'We're leaving, Isobel.'

But still Isobel didn't move. 'Don't you think at least you should have discussed this with *me* before you came to your decision?'

Orlando froze, half standing up from the table,

incredulity clawing at his composure. Had he heard her right?

'Discuss it with *you*?' He hissed the words.

'Yes.'

'And why, exactly, would I do that?'

'Well…' A flush crept up Isobel's neck but still she held her ground, refusing to blink against his barely leashed anger. 'Because of our unborn child, of course.' She drew in a sharp breath. 'I mean, obviously we don't know yet whether we will have a boy, but if we do it's hardly fair to dispose of his inheritance like this just because *you* don't want it.'

Orlando's voice was lethally low as he leant forward to hold his face up close to Isobel's. 'You have no idea what you are talking about, Isobel. I suggest you drop this conversation—*now.*'

His every instinct was telling him to grab hold of her hand, lead her away from the curious eyes of the other diners and into the street, where he would silence her himself in the way he'd been dying to do this whole evening. With a punishing kiss. One that would drive all thoughts of titles and inheritances out of her mind and leave her begging for mercy. Or begging for more.

But Isobel wasn't done yet. In fact it seemed the more his anger simmered so dangerously between them, the more determined she was to make it burst into flames.

'Well, what about your father, then?'

It was as if a wall of ice-cold water had sluiced over Orlando—as if he had stepped beneath a waterfall—pounding in his ears and tightening every muscle in his body.

'What *about* him?'

The glinting malice in his voice should have told her to back right off, but not Isobel. Pure stubbornness made her continue. 'How do you think *he* would feel about you selling the estate? After all, by leaving it to you in his will wasn't he entrusting you with its safekeeping?'

'Ha!' With a cruel laugh Orlando dropped back down in his seat, his breath trapped high in his chest. He paused, waiting for the surge of fury to abate. He had to make himself control this reaction, tamp down the anger in his voice. 'You have no idea how ridiculous that assumption is, Isobel. For your information, my father is the reason I am selling the estate—the reason I want nothing whatsoever to do with it.'

Isobel's thick dark lashes lowered as she processed this information. 'Can I ask why?'

Orlando glared back at her. He wanted to say no, she couldn't. He wanted never to have to speak of the man again, to erase him from his life, cleanse him from his soul. Something he thought he had done until this inheritance had reared up to grab him by the throat, brought him back to Trevente to open up the festering wounds. But Isobel was still watching him, waiting for an explanation.

'Because my father was scum, Isobel. The vilest of creatures. A man whose depravity knew no bounds.'

Isobel visibly tensed, her shock at his vicious statement showing in her eyes. When she finally spoke her voice trembled with emotion.

'What did he do, Orlando? Whatever did he do that was so bad?'

The scowl that marred Orlando's brow was deep enough to narrow his eyes to glinting slits of stone.

'He murdered someone, Isobel.' His words came out in a muted roar. 'Is that bad enough for you?'

CHAPTER FIVE

ORLANDO WATCHED WITH something strangely akin to satisfaction as the shock of his revelation swept across Isobel's face, opening her mouth, shining like glass in her eyes.

He had always loved the expressiveness of her face, the way her every thought, every reaction gave away her innermost feelings—at least until she had the chance to cover them up. He watched her trying to do just that now—trying to hide the smack of shock that had drained the colour from her cheeks. But she couldn't manage it. Not this time.

Gone was the bolshie attitude, the softly persuasive look and the irritating beginnings of sympathy, to be replaced with appalled confusion. Now she looked at him the way he deserved. She looked at him as if he was the son of a murderer.

'I need to get some air, Orlando. It's very hot in here.' Pushing back her chair, Isobel rose unsteadily to her feet.

'Of course.'

Moving the table, he watched as she edged her way out, apologising and thanking the other diners in that oh-so-English way. Then, with an arm around her shoulder, he shepherded her out into the relative cool of the night air.

'Do you feel unwell?' Shame gripped him as he looked down on her slight, vulnerable figure. This was all *his* doing. Isobel was pregnant with his child—he should be looking after her, protecting her, not burdening her with his despicable family secrets.

Collecting herself, Isobel took a deep breath, then a step back to free herself from his arm. 'I'll be fine in a minute.'

She looked over Orlando's shoulder, then down at her feet—anywhere, Orlando realised, rather than at him.

'The car's not far away. Can you walk there?'

'Yes, of course.'

Self-hatred made Orlando start off at a brisk pace until, remembering Isobel's frailty—not to mention those wretched boots—he moderated his step. Isobel paced beside him, unnervingly silent. He had expected a barrage of unwelcome questions, had been prepared to give her the bare minimum of details about his father before announcing that the subject was closed—*for ever*. But this silence was worse...far worse.

Shooting her a sideways glance, he could see she was lost in thought, oblivious to the streets that had held such charm for her earlier in the evening. As the breeze blew her shiny hair back from her face he could make out the hollows of her cheekbones, darkly shadowed by the unworldly orange glow of the street lights.

By the time they reached the car, parked on a narrow pavement right up against a wall, Isobel had still not uttered a word, and any perverted sense of satisfaction Orlando might have initially felt had been replaced with a gnawing sense of acceptance and shame. Now she knew the sort of blood that their child would inherit Isobel had gone into shock. And who could blame her?

'Wait here and I'll pull the car out so that you can get in.'

He was opening the driver's door, about to get behind the wheel, when Isobel finally spoke.

'There's no need, I can slide across.'

Turning to look at her, Orlando took in the pale anguish that was etched across her face. And it twisted his heart.

'Just as you like.'

Standing back, he watched as she lowered herself into the driver's seat, swinging those long, booted legs over the gearstick to get to the passenger side and revealing a tantalising glimpse of naked thigh as she did so.

Orlando suppressed the immediate jerk of lust. After all, by refusing to stand in the street and wait for him to pull the car out, what exactly was she saying? That she was worried he was setting her up as a target? That he intended to mow her down in cold blood, right here and now, solving the problem of her pregnancy with the rush of cold metal and the screech of tyres? Maybe she thought murder was in his genes. Like father like son.

Certainly he was feeling pretty murderous now.

Starting up the engine, Orlando let the car roar into life, navigating it bumpily through the cobbled streets until they eventually joined the coastal road that led back to the hotel.

Beside him Isobel sat ramrod-straight, gripping on to the seat belt across her chest with one hand and the side of the leather seat with the other. She broke her silence only to ask him to slow down, in a voice that croaked with fear. It seemed she had no more faith in his driving than she did in his character. Or maybe the two were connected.

So their half-hour journey back to the hotel was travelled in a death-like hush, with just the hum of the engine and the whistle of the wind for company as both parties stared fixedly at the dark road that snaked before them.

Finally back at the hotel, Isobel sank down on to the sofa and gulped down a large glass of water. She was exhausted, but she couldn't go to bed—not until she had talked to Orlando, made some sense of what he'd told her.

But first she needed to steady her nerves…reclaim her stomach from where it had been left behind, somewhere on one of those horrendous hairpin bends. The journey back from Trevente had been horrific, but she had survived it. In fact the masterful ease with which Orlando had dealt with the extreme cornering had strangely given her a bit more confidence—like some sort of aversion therapy.

Now, as she surveyed the man before her, she felt her poor stomach knot for an entirely different reason. After shrugging off his jacket he had rolled up his sleeves and was now pouring himself a large whisky, noisily dropping in several cubes of ice. He looked dark and brooding and distracted as he moved around the room, but also slightly vulnerable. And it was *that* that tugged at Isobel's heartstrings, made her want to reach out to him both physically and emotionally.

'It's getting late.' Orlando seated himself on the sofa opposite her, his laptop on his knees. 'You should get to bed.'

Isobel stared across at him, judging how to continue. She knew she was going to have to be careful or Orlando would retreat behind his fortress of privacy, pull up the drawbridge and leave her standing on the wrong side.

'We need to talk first.'

'Not now.' Opening his laptop, Orlando took a sip of his drink, balancing the glass on the arm of the sofa. 'I've got some work to do—things

I need to attend to before the New York office closes.'

'Well, they will have to wait.' Standing up, Isobel crossed the room and seated herself beside him, reaching across to close the laptop. *So much for being careful*. 'This is more important.'

Orlando shot her a look of sharp surprise. 'I don't take orders from you, Isobel.' His fingers went to open the laptop again but then, changing his mind, he placed it on the floor and shoved it to one side with his foot before turning to face her. 'Or anyone else, for that matter.'

Too close now, Isobel was caught in the crossfire of his contemptuous stare. 'Well, what do you expect?' She tipped up her chin. 'That you can announce that your father is a murderer and then say no more about it?'

Saying the word *murderer* out loud made it seem impossibly, horribly real. It hung above them like a guillotine blade. But at least she had got Orlando's full attention—in all its skin-scorching glory.

She swallowed, lowering her voice. 'Don't you at least think you owe me an explanation?'

'I owe you nothing, Isobel. Least of all an explanation of my past.'

Isobel stared at him, past the barked reply to the muscle that twitched beneath a cheek shadowed with stubble. He was hurting—she could see that. Suddenly she longed to take that rough chin in her hands, position her lips over his and use their warm pout to release that tightly drawn line, make them soften, make them *hers*. But she would do no such thing. Not unless she wanted to suffer the sting of rejection.

'In any case—' he attempted a throwaway remark '—you are better off not knowing.'

Isobel shook her head. 'It's too late for that, Orlando.' She pushed herself back against the sofa and crossed her arms. 'I'm not going anywhere until you tell me what your father did.'

There was a long moment when their eyes clashed, before Orlando reached for his glass and took a deep slug. 'Very well, if that's the way you want it. But don't say I didn't warn you.' Getting up, he went to refill his glass, waving the heavy decanter at Isobel. 'D'you want to join me? You may need it.'

Isobel shook her head. As Orlando loomed before her again, looking down at her with eyes as black as midnight, she felt a shiver of dread at what he was about to reveal, felt her hands beginning to tremble as he sat down beside her.

'I have already told you that my father—the last Marchese di Trevente—was the lowest possible form of human life.' Orlando began his character assassination of his father with all the calmness of a contract killer, staring straight ahead, avoiding Isobel's searching gaze. 'A dishonourable, cheating liar who abandoned my mother when she needed him most and refused to even acknowledge my existence.'

Despite the grim acceptance, the facade of indifference, Isobel could hear the rawness in his voice—could sense how hard it was for him to talk about this. She wanted to take his hand in hers, offer some sort of comfort, but instinct—or self-preservation—kept them firmly twisting in her lap.

'But it wasn't until I was seventeen, when I foolishly decided to seek him out, that I saw for myself what a monster he truly was. He used me, Isobel, and then betrayed me—the same way he had my mother...the same way he did anyone who was unfortunate enough to cross his path.'

'How did he do that?' She posed the question tentatively, conscious that Orlando might clam up any moment, refuse to reveal any more.

'He told me he had a plan—something that I could help him with.' Orlando shifted in his seat. 'And, being the reckless youngster that I was, I went along with it—at least until I came to my senses. He said he needed money—a lot of it and fast—which wasn't surprising, considering he'd managed to gamble and drink his way through his inheritance and let the entire estate go to ruin. His plan was to burn down the Cassano wine warehouse on the docks here in Trevente and claim on the insurance. I'd get my cut. Tempting to a young man like me who literally had nothing.'

'I'm sure.'

'So initially I agreed.' He took another slug of whisky, turning to face Isobel full-on. 'A big mistake.'

Isobel bit down hard on her lip. 'But you said you came to your senses… You didn't actually go through with it?'

'No. I told him I'd changed my mind. So he set about doing it himself. Razed the place to the ground.'

Isobel saw Orlando's throat move, his knuckles white on the hand that gripped the glass. Everything about his stiffly held body, his tortured expression, told her that something bad—something *very* bad—had happened. She waited, both willing him to continue and dreading what she might hear.

'There was someone in the warehouse…a girl. Sophia—the daughter of a wine merchant.' His voiced dropped low. 'She was overcome by smoke. I managed to drag her out but it was too late. They couldn't revive her.'

'Oh, God, Orlando, that's awful.' Isobel's hand flew to her throat. 'But to accuse your father of *murder*, Orlando…that's a very strong word.' Isobel found herself desperately—stupidly—trying to lessen the shock for herself and ease the anguish for Orlando. 'Surely it was a tragic accident? He had no idea she was in there.'

'Murder, manslaughter—call it what you like. The fact is he killed Sophia as surely as if he'd plunged a knife into her chest.'

Orlando's tormented expression ripped through Isobel.

'And the courts agreed.' Collecting himself now, he continued. 'He got fifteen years. That was despite his best efforts to pin the blame on *me*, of course.'

'He did that?'

'Yep. Honourable to the last, my father.'

'How dreadful for you.' Isobel flinched against the idea that a man could do such a thing to his son. 'Did he die in prison?'

'No. He was released a few years ago, but he knew better than to try and make contact with me. He never returned to Trevente either. He's back here now, of course—in a coffin.'

There was a long pause.

'I'm so sorry, Orlando.'

'What is there for *you* to be sorry about?' Suddenly rough, Orlando scowled at her. 'None of this is any of your concern. The man is dead now. His wretched past can be buried with him.'

So that was it—the reason Orlando was so determined to renounce the title of Marchese di Trevente and sell the estate. Isobel scanned the taut features of his face, trying to make sense of what he had told her. Because something didn't add up. Orlando was a planner, a strategist— surely he would have decided long ago what he was going to do with the Trevente estate when he inherited it. Why did his reaction feel so immediate? So raw?

She decided to risk another question. 'You must have known that this would be your inheritance. Did you always plan to sell it?'

'I knew nothing of the sort. When I defied my father he took great delight in telling me that I would get nothing. Like I cared. Nothing would have been infinitely preferable.'

'And yet he left it to you anyway?'

'I can only think it was his way of having the last laugh.' Orlando roughly raked a hand through his hair. 'Leaving me an estate that he had managed to bring to its knees and a title that's synonymous with an alcoholic, gambling murderer.'

'I see.' In the chilling quiet of the room an idea suddenly formed in Isobel's head. 'Will you take me there?'

'Scusi?'

'Will you take me to the Trevente estate to see the *castello*? If you really are determined to sell it, this will be my only chance.'

'Why on earth would you want to see it?'

'So I can get some sense of the history of your

family before it's lost for ever. So I can describe it to our child in the future, when he or she asks about their heritage.'

'Spare me the violins, please.' Getting to his feet, Orlando looked down on her with merciless scorn. 'Much as I hate to burst your rosy bubble, there is nothing about the place that you would want to describe to our child. The *castello* has been lying empty for the last seventeen years. It was in an appalling state then—I dread to think what it looks like now.'

'I want to see it, Orlando.'

Isobel watched as her fierce determination met his wall of resistance. She saw his eyes flicker, then narrow, his throat move as he deliberated.

'Very well. If you insist.'

'Can we go tomorrow?'

'Tomorrow…whenever—it makes no difference to me.'

'Thank you, Orlando.' Isobel gave him a genuine smile. 'I appreciate it.'

Isobel stared up in awe at the majestic old building that towered before them. With its single turret flanking rows of shuttered windows it was like a fairy tale castle, standing tall and proud against the cobalt blue of the evening sky.

But it was certainly in one hell of a state. Ivy scrambled across the honey-coloured stone, creeping over the shutters and the ornate iron balconies. Large chunks of masonry had fallen away and the row of architectural balustrades high above them were tipping drunkenly against one another. The shallow flight of steps that Orlando was marching up now was almost covered with weeds and tangled undergrowth.

Picking her way carefully to join him, Isobel stood under the crumbling portico of the massive front door, taking in the peeling, sun-bleached paint and the circular bronze knocker as Orlando forced the heavy iron key into the lock.

Inside the *castello* it was dark and musty-smelling. Isobel stood in the hallway, waiting for her eyes to acclimatise, but Orlando had already made for one of the many doorways, striding towards it and flinging open the door. She could hear his footsteps echoing across the wooden floor, and her eyes followed him as he crossed the cavernous room, tugging at the metal catch that opened the shutters and pushing them back with an unnecessary force that saw them creaking against their rusty hinges.

Moving to the doorway, she watched as he went over to the next set of shutters, flinging them open in the same aggressive way before marching over to the third.

'We need to get some light in this place.' His voice was a growl over his shoulder.

Feeling a switch beside her, Isobel flicked it down, looking up hopefully at the two enormous, dusty chandeliers that hung high above them from a ceiling gaping with holes. But there was nothing. And despite Orlando's feverish attempts, even with the shutters open, little of the setting sun's light permeated and the room was still bathed in a dusky grey twilight.

Narrowing her eyes, Isobel tried to take in the scene around her. Dust sheets of various shapes and sizes concealed pieces of furniture like weary ghosts, and massive portraits in crumbling gilt frames adorned the walls—along with darkened rectangles on the ripped silk wallpaper where others had hung. The far end of the room was dominated by a carved marble fireplace, its grate blackened by centuries of roaring fires.

When her eyes finally came back to Orlando, Isobel realised he had been watching her intently, a look of grim satisfaction on his face.

'So.' Standing with his back to the window, feet planted wide apart and arms folded, he addressed her with calculated ruthlessness. 'Now you have seen my inheritance for yourself, has it shattered your romantic image?'

Isobel shook her head, slowly advancing towards him, still looking around her. 'I think it's beautiful, Orlando.'

'Hah!' Orlando's scornful reply echoed around

them. 'Then you have a very strange idea of beauty, Isobel. I don't see anything very beautiful about this—' he kicked at a large piece of plasterwork that had fallen by his feet '—or *this*.' Marching over to the fireplace he gestured at the remains of a blackbird, long dead.

Isobel shuddered. 'What I mean is I can see that it was beautiful once and could be beautiful again.'

She watched Orlando walk away from the bird before he returned his punishing stare to her face. But she wasn't going to back down. Filling her lungs to continue speaking, she could hear a small inner voice asking her just why she felt the need to defend this place so strongly—especially in the face of Orlando's obvious hostility. For some reason she wanted to protect it—somehow it had already stolen her heart.

'I think that with time and money and vision this place could be restored to its former glory and would make an absolutely stunning ancestral home.'

'*Do* you, now?' Sarcasm leached from his words.

'Yes, I do. And if *I* had inherited this property—if it had been in *my* family for generations—I wouldn't dream of selling it. No matter what...' She hesitated, knowing she was straying into dangerous territory. 'No matter what had happened in the recent past.'

'Is that so?'

The sneer in Orlando's voice scraped her skin as he closed the space between them, standing before her with blazing contempt in his eyes.

'What *is* it with you, Isobel? Why are you so interested in this place? Do you fancy yourself as a *marchesa*? Is that it? I know the English are obsessed with their titles.'

'No—it's nothing whatsoever to do with that!' Isobel smarted. 'And may I remind you that in order to be the Marchesa I would have to be your wife?'

'And so you will be.' Orlando's voice was a decisive lash across the quiet of the room.

'Oh, you think so, do you? I wouldn't be so sure.'

Bristling at his overbearing authority, Isobel tossed the contemptuous words at him. Then immediately wished she hadn't. Because the murderous look on Orlando's face, along with the dramatic drop in temperature, sent a trickle of ice through her veins, raising the hairs on the back of her neck. In the dying light even the shrouded furniture seemed to have awoken to her reckless words, as if the spirits beneath were shifting.

'You gave me your word, Isobel…' Orlando's voice was a low, deadly, growl.

As he leant forward Isobel felt her breath shudder to a halt, only to be released in a gasp when he reached for a lock of her hair.

'I wouldn't recommend changing your mind

now.' He let the silky softness of her hair slip between his fingers, watching as it fell to frame her face. 'I think that would be a very bad idea indeed.'

'I didn't say I had changed my mind.' With his eyes mercilessly tracing every inch of her startled face, Isobel fought to stand her ground. 'But neither will I give in to threats.'

'Well, that makes two of us, Isobel. Because if you think you can use marriage as some sort of bargaining tool, to give you some sort of hold over me, then you are very much mistaken. For the sake of our child we *are* going to be married. And that's an end to it.'

Isobel stared back at him, refusing to be cowed. But he was too close, too alive—just too hypnotically, magnetically Orlando. As his gaze probed hers, his breath soft and warm on her face, all her thoughts of a clever comeback were lost. Instead she had to fight the electrifying jolt of awareness that was hammering through her. Silently cursing herself, she lowered her head.

'So.' Taking her silence as a sign of victory, Orlando placed a finger under her chin and raised her face to meet his again. 'If not for the title, tell me why you are so keen to protect my inheritance?'

Isobel blinked against his stare. She really had no idea.

'Why does this crumbling ruin of a place ex-

cite you when my attempts to offer you a beautiful home in New York are shot down in flames?'

'I don't know what you're talking about. I...'

'Then let me elaborate.' He pressed a fingertip
to her lips. 'You treat our relationship—whatever
the hell *that* is—like some sort of business deal
that you have to endure. You try and exclude me
from being a part of my baby's life. You deliberately construct barriers to keep me out. And if that
weren't enough you question every damned decision I make—whether it's to do with the marriage
or the baby or even this rotting pile of bricks. In
short, you contest everything I say.'

'No, I don't.'

It was almost funny—it *would* have been funny
if she hadn't been pinned to the spot by Orlando's
punishing stare, aware of the angry rasp of his
breath. Moving his head fractionally to one side,
he raised dark brows in a gesture that showed how
neatly she had fallen into his trap.

Isobel touched her tingling lip with the tip of
her tongue—a gesture that saw his eyes blaze with
fire, then narrow.

'So what are you saying? That you expect me
to take orders from you? Basically do as I'm told?
Because, if so, I can tell you that is *never* going
to happen.'

'Evidently.' Orlando rubbed at his eyes with a
spanned hand.

'Anyway, I could say the same of you. You insist on challenging all *my* decisions.' Sensing that he was weakening, if not exactly on the ropes, and that he was tiring of this subject, Isobel went in with a final jab. 'Maybe we are as bad as each other.'

'Yes. Maybe we are.' With one last telling stare Orlando jammed his hands into his pockets and turned away. 'Come on. We are leaving.'

'Leaving?' Isobel repeated.

'I've seen enough.'

'But we've only just got here. We haven't even been upstairs yet, or seen the grounds or anything.'

'I said I've seen enough.'

Moving past her, he swept out into the hall, obviously thinking that the force of his black mood alone would be enough to sweep her along in his wake. Well, he could think again. She certainly wasn't going to get into a car with him when he was behaving like this. It was too dangerous. He'd drive too fast. She was going nowhere right now.

'I'm staying here.' Conscious of her contrary image, Isobel thought she might as well live up to it.

'*Scusi?*' Orlando swung round to face her again, his features blackened by irritation. If he'd been wearing a cape it would have been swept across his body in a show of contempt.

'I said I want to stay here a bit longer.' Straightening her spine, Isobel refused to weaken under his blistering gaze. 'I'll get a taxi back to the hotel if you don't want to wait.'

'And how exactly do you intend to do that?'

'Easy.' She delved into her bag for her phone, but what Orlando's smug silence suggested was soon confirmed by the screen—there was absolutely no signal. 'Well, when you get back to the hotel you could arrange for a taxi to pick me up in an hour or so.'

'I could.' Orlando's voice was now an infuriating growl. 'But I have no intention of doing any such thing.'

Isobel balled her fists by her side. Why did he always have to call the shots? Why did everything have to be done on Orlando Cassano's terms?

'Look. If you go ahead with your threat to sell Castello Trevente this may be my one and only chance to have a look around. So if you don't mind, since we're here, I'm going to take the opportunity to see what's upstairs.'

In a gesture of pure defiance she turned away from him, starting up the stairs before he had the chance to stop her.

'Just as you like.' Isobel didn't need to see his face to know that Orlando's tight words of concession were killing him. 'You've got ten minutes.'

Ten minutes. As she continued her stately ascent of the stairs, picking her way over fallen masonry, she mentally told him what he could do with his ten minutes. She was going to stay here as long as she wanted. What could he do about it? Drag her out by her hair?

Isobel quickly banished that image from her mind before it sank its erotic claws into her skin.

'And by the way...' Orlando called up to her retreating back. 'Selling this place is not a threat. Now that I've seen the state of it I can tell you—it's a certainty.'

CHAPTER SIX

MARCHING AROUND THE overgrown gardens, Orlando checked his watch yet again. Isobel's ten minutes had stretched into fifteen, twenty, and there was still no sign of her. He'd go in there and demand she came out if he had to—and that was looking increasingly likely—but throwing his weight around wasn't his style. At least it never had been.

Orlando was no longer sure about anything any more. How had he ended up here, in the place he'd vowed he would never revisit, with a woman he barely knew who was carrying his child? What the hell had happened to his life?

Returning to Castello Trevente had been a mistake. He should never have come back. The memories of that fateful summer, those few weeks when he had lived here, had come flooding back like a dark tide as soon as he had driven through the iron gates at the entrance to the estate. Only a sideways glance at Isobel's tight-lipped determination had stopped him from turning the car around there and then, and roaring away in the opposite direction.

Inside the *castello* the ghosts of the past had been waiting for him, just as he had known they would be. He recalled the sense of wonder he'd had on his first visit, so excited about the new life that had been opened up to him. Wonder that had turned to boredom and then impatience as he had roamed around the deserted *castello* in search of something to do, ending up camping in one room as he waited for his father to join him.

It hadn't taken Orlando long to realise that Carlo Cassano much preferred the anonymous gambling dens and drinking holes of Bologna or Milan to the tiresome responsibilities that awaited his attention on the Trevente estate. The live-in staff of the *castello* had long since departed, but there had still been the tenant farmers, the vineyards and the olive groves, all desperately needing his attention.

When his father had finally turned up it hadn't been to address any of those issues. His only interest had been the criminal plan he was masterminding and persuading Orlando, his long-lost son, to do his bidding.

In the meantime Orlando had met Sophia, the pretty daughter of a local wine merchant. Sophia had been banned from seeing Orlando by her father—no doubt because of Orlando's wild ways and the debauched reputation of his father—but their romance had flourished in secret, fuelled by the naivety of youth and the thrill of illicit love.

The Cassano wine warehouse had been their secret meeting place. Cool, dark and with the rich smell of alcohol and aged oak, it had seemed like the perfect hideaway. And it was there that they had planned to meet that fateful night—the night when everything had changed.

Getting ready to leave the *castello*, Orlando had been waylaid by the arrival of his father. Drunk and waving a fistful of notes, Carlo Cassano had come crashing in, announcing that this was a down payment for Orlando, that more riches would be coming his way once Orlando had done his work and the warehouse had been reduced to ashes. But the sight of his slurring father had turned Orlando's stomach, and suddenly he had realised that he could never go through with this crazy idea.

So he had told Carlo that the deal was off, that he wouldn't be carrying out his criminal plan after all. A vicious, furious row had ensued, echoing through the empty rooms, sending birds screeching from the rafters and shattering the stagnant peace of the *castello*. Snarling with hatred, Carlo Cassano had started to swing his fists, all the while hurling abuse at his 'spineless and pathetic' son. Easily blocking the drunken punches, Orlando had felt their blows nevertheless—to his dignity and his pride—and had faced the hideous reality that he was the son of such a man.

Watching him storm off into the night, Orlando had done nothing to stop him, only too glad to see the back of him. And that was the moment that Orlando would regret for the rest of his life.

For instead of leaving for the warehouse there and then—going to meet Sophia as planned—Orlando had waited an hour. He'd needed time to stop the adrenaline pumping through his body—time to let his temper die down and for the utter disgust and revulsion he felt for his father to fade, so he could unclench his fists and loosen his clenched jaw.

Unbeknownst to Orlando, his father had gone straight to the warehouse, having decided to carry out his evil plan himself that very night. It was only when word had reached Orlando that the warehouse was on fire that he'd realised with full sickening horror what had happened.

Racing down to the docks, he had thrown himself into the smoke-filled inferno, oblivious to the searing heat and the flying glass of exploding wine bottles, desperately hoping against hope that he was wrong—that Sophia wasn't in there at all, but safe somewhere, far away from this hell.

All hope had been extinguished when he'd found her and realised that he was too late. Sophia had already died. And Orlando had had to live with the weight of that on his conscience ever since.

Marching his temper around as he'd waited for Isobel, Orlando had found himself in the Cassano family graveyard, face to face with his father's grave. Staring at the newly dug earth, at the grave still waiting for its headstone, he had felt nothing but revulsion, and the surge of anger had been enough to tense every muscle in his body, burn the backs of his eyes.

What the hell was he doing here?

Bending down to pick up a fallen branch, Orlando scythed it from side to side, attacking the weeds that had grown in rampant profusion all around.

And where the hell was Isobel?

He slashed at the long grass, beheading scarlet poppies. This young woman was in danger of seriously winding him up—no, correction, she had already done that...with bells on. Orlando cursed himself for letting Isobel get to him. He had no idea why he'd given vent to that outburst of frustration back in the drawing room, why he had felt the need to point out how infuriating he found her. It wasn't as if it had done any good. It had simply exposed his weakness and given her the chance to demonstrate that sheer bloody-mindedness that she epitomised so well.

He thought back to the way she had looked as she had stood there in the half-light: boldly defiant, sassy, sexy. His eyes had been drawn to the swell of her breasts, grown more full as a result of her pregnancy, straining against the pale green fabric of her sundress. It had been all he could do not to reach out for her, to pull her against his growing arousal, let her see for herself what she did to him.

How she did it, Orlando had no idea. Sure, she

was beautiful—but then he had known a lot of beautiful women in his life. There was something about her, a fresh-faced loveliness, that made him want to keep on looking, to drink her in until his tortured body was drowned in lust. Even when she had deliberately disobeyed him, marching up the stairs when he had expressly told her they were leaving, he had wanted to halt her progress with the span of his hands, to grip that pert backside and grind her against his need. To do *something*—anything—to alleviate his blood-pumping, groin-tightening, rampant desire.

Basically, the woman drove him crazy. And, worse still, the cravings he was so desperately trying to control were being met with a cool disregard, the whole ice-queen routine. It felt as if she was deliberately taunting him, determined to shake his self-control.

Well, congratulations, Ms Spicer. Snapping the branch across his knee, Orlando flung it into the bushes and marched back towards the house. *You have succeeded.* Taking the steps two at a time he flung open the front door and strode across the hall. *But just maybe you will wish that you hadn't.*

Reaching the galleried landing, he paused to steady his breath, holding on to a banister that wobbled beneath his grip. Rooms led off in all directions but only one door was open, and it was there that he made for, driven on by a determination that he couldn't articulate but which surged through him, firing the blood in his veins.

Isobel was standing in front of the window when he marched in, obstinately refusing to turn even though she couldn't have failed to hear his stamping approach. Her slender frame was held perfectly still, silhouetted against a sky slashed with the orange and red streaks of a stunning sunset. She appeared transfixed, as if the colours had caught her in their spell. A spell that Orlando obviously had no chance of breaking, despite taking several steps closer, despite the sound of his agitated breath rasping through the still air.

'Isobel!'

Turning to face him, she held a finger to her lips and that wound him up even more. She'd got some nerve, this one. Not only had she kept him waiting, now she had the barefaced cheek to tell him to keep quiet when he had been forced to come and find her. But that was Isobel all over, wasn't it? Ignoring his orders, disobeying his instructions, treating him with an offhand disregard that was deliberately designed to try and undermine him. Well, they would see about that…

Closing the space between them, Orlando stood right behind her, so close that her floral scent invaded his nostrils and his shortened breath moved the strands of hair on the top of her head. He felt the familiar jolt of awareness pass between them and it brought a gleam of satisfaction to his eye. *Oh, yes.* Isobel might try and deny her attraction to him with her haughty disregard, the whole you-mean-nothing-to-me routine, but her body was betraying her now—just has he had planned it would.

He could sense rather than see the way she had stiffened, and knew that every nerve ending was alert to his presence despite the fact that she hadn't moved a muscle. Or maybe because of it. He could just raise his hand, sweep the glossy curtain of hair to one side, lower his lips to the nape of her neck and see how she liked that. Run his lips slowly up the pale, soft skin to her ear lobe and wait for her to tremble beneath his hot breath. And then…

And then nothing. Because he wasn't going to do it. Because this erotic fantasy was in danger of backfiring—big time. Because he could already feel the tightening of lust swelling in his groin, pushing aside all rational thought and demanding to be acted upon. And that wasn't what he was supposed to be doing here. He was supposed to be testing Isobel, making her see that her icy facade didn't fool him for one moment, making her realise that she could be his whenever he wanted. That he could make her beg for mercy, scream his name and plead with him to take her there and then, any way he wanted.

What he *wasn't* supposed to be doing was demonstrating his own complete lack of control, letting her see the infuriating, all-consuming power she seemed to have over him. If it took every ounce of will power that he possessed he would prevent that.

'I told you ten minutes.'

'Look.'

Reluctantly Orlando let his gaze follow Isobel's pointed finger to the scene through the window. In the low light of dusk he could see a herd of deer grazing in the overgrown wilderness that had once been formal gardens. No more than about thirty yards away, they seemed perfectly at ease, proud stags with their impressive antlers held high, females watching over their young, the distinctive dappling on the backs of the fawns still visible. Every now and then there would be a flash of white as a deer's rump caught the last rays of the failing light.

'Aren't they beautiful?'

'*Caprioli*. Roe deer.' Despite himself Orlando found he had lowered his voice, was speaking softly against the back of her hair.

'Do they belong to you?'

'I have no idea.' Rousing himself from the delights of the bucolic scene, Orlando hardened his heart. 'But if they do now they won't much longer.'

This retort saw Isobel finally spin around, her eyes glittering as she spanned her hands across his chest to push him away—or to prevent him from moving. Orlando didn't know which. Either way, he could feel their heat through the cotton of his shirt.

'You surprise me, Orlando.' Isobel's eyes darkened to an ocean-green with the graze of his puckered nipples beneath her fingers and it made her drop her arms by her sides. 'I would never have put you down as the sort of man who would run away from anything.'

'*Chiedo scusa?* I beg your pardon?'

'That's what you're doing, you know. You are running away from your past.' Tipping back her head, she confronted him full-on. 'You would rather see a home that has been in your family for generations sold to a hotel chain or razed to the ground than have to face up to what happened with your father.'

'That's enough!' Orlando's voice rumbled around the darkening room like thunder. Raking a murderous gaze across her upturned face, he took in the flushed cheeks, the wilful glint in her eyes. Something fluttered inside him at the sight of those long, dark lashes brushing her cheeks. 'I will *not* stand here listening to your half-baked theories about my character and my motives.'

'Why? Because you are afraid they might be true?'

There was a long, dangerous silence. Boy, she was really pushing it now. Orlando waited for his fury to abate, waited until he was sure he had full control of voice.

'You are forgetting your place, Isobel. You may be carrying my child, but that's where it ends. You do not interfere in my affairs. And you do not speak to me like that. *Ever.*'

'Well, somebody has to.' Still she refused to back down, but his sharp rebuke had brought a tremor to her voice. 'Someone needs to stop you selling the Trevente estate and losing it for ever. Someone needs to make you see that you are not thinking straight right now.'

'So you know what I am thinking, do you, Isobel?' Lowering his head, Orlando hissed his words quietly against Isobel's ear. 'Come on, then. If you are so clever, what I am thinking right now?'

'Don't be ridiculous, Orlando.' Isobel turned to move away but, grasping hold of her wrists, Orlando held her firm.

'If you know so much about me…if you are so sure that you can read my mind…tell me, Isobel. I'd be interested to know.'

His lips grazed the skin just below her ear and he felt her angle her head against the light pressure. *Dio*, she tasted so good. He squeezed her wrists tighter.

'I have absolutely no idea.' The words were boldly delivered but she didn't pull away.

'Really?' Moving his mouth slowly down her

neck, he kept his touch deliberately light, dry with the heat of his breath. His lips were soft, dragging against the silky smoothness of her skin, opening against the downward movement but exerting no pressure of their own. *Not yet.*

Isobel twitched against him. He was at the base of her throat now, in the delectable hollow between her collarbones. He let his tongue slip out, lightly circle the indentation before withdrawing again. 'So, are you figuring it out yet?'

'Orlando, you need to stop this...'

'Not very impressive, if you don't mind my saying.' Tipping back his head just enough to find her eyes, Orlando held her trance-like gaze, watching as the emerald sparks of denial melted into a sea-green swirl of arousal that she couldn't control. He felt his heart rate spike wildly, telling himself that this was vindication. Nothing whatsoever to do with his own rampant longing.

'For someone who professes to be so intuitive, you are telling me you aren't feeling anything now?'

'No.' Isobel tipped back her head, the better to expose her throat to his lips, the movement shifting her hips towards his, brushing against the ache in his groin. 'Absolutely nothing.'

Hmm... Was she playing with him? Because he sure as hell wasn't fooled by that throwaway remark.

'Then I will just have to try harder.'

Raising his head so that he looked down into her face, he let his eyes rest there for a second, enjoying the moment. Then all at once his hands were in her hair, plunging into the velvety softness, his fingers threading through the tresses to pull her towards him. He just caught sight of her lips opening—whether in protest or invitation he didn't know or care, because he was going to claim those lips for his own either way. He was going to kiss the hell out of her right now, whether she wanted it or not. *That* was a certainty.

He covered her mouth with his own, capturing it with a force that surprised even himself, but he had no intention of tempering it. They were playing a game here, right? She was testing him, goading him to try to arouse her, to make her eat her words. Well, it would be his pleasure. And judging by the way her body was reacting, arching against his rather than pushing him away, and the way her lips were opening beneath his to allow him to plunder within, rather than pursing shut, it was going to be a piece of cake.

Increasing the pressure still further, he revelled in the damp heat of her mouth, her breath hot and sweet against the rush of his own, betraying her desire. And as his tongue flicked feverishly around, seeking hers, he was finally rewarded when it curled against his, firm and erotic, and more than enough to shoot a bolt of sexual intensity to his core.

Pulling her even more firmly against him, Orlando held her prisoner with fingers that were still threaded through her hair.

'And now?'

Releasing her lips to allow a rasping intake of breath, he growled the question urgently against her cheek. He knew he had given up any hope of restraining the desire that was now raging through his body—that at this moment he had no idea who was testing whom. It was a wildly liberating realisation. He was free to do whatever he wanted.

'Are you telling me you still feel nothing?'

'Orlando, I...'

'You what, Isobel? You want more convincing?'

Staring down at her flushed cheeks, her eyes bright with excitement, her chest heaving from the force of their kiss, Orlando knew with a satisfied certainty that she was going to have trouble getting out of this one. The pedant in him looked forward to hearing her try. The male in him needed her to make it quick.

'One kiss means nothing, Orlando.' She gave him a quick upward glance. 'It doesn't signify anything.'

But despite her coolly delivered words Orlando knew that Isobel Spicer was hanging on to her composure with fingertips that were fast losing their grip on the ledge. And that brought the curve of a smile to his lips.

'Is that so? So no doubt this won't mean anything either.' Moving one arm around her slender waist, he twisted her body, hooking his other arm under the backs of her knees to sweep her effortlessly off her feet.

'Orlando!'

Instinctively her arms flew around his neck to steady herself, which suited Orlando fine as he was moving now, across the echoing room that he had barely registered until now, marching towards the large shrouded shape in the middle of the floor that had to be a bed—or if it wasn't it would have to serve as one. With Isobel clinging on to him, her body bumping against his, arousing him more and more with each jerky step, he knew that he didn't care what was under that cloth so long as he could throw Isobel down on it—with himself on top.

'Orlando, put me down.' Her breath was hot against his neck, the fingers that had found their way beneath his collar digging into the skin of his shoulders with delicious pain.

'I intend to.'

The white shape was in front of them now—a looming iceberg in the gloom of the room. Releasing one arm from Isobel's body for long enough to be able to grab at the dust sheet, Orlando watched with satisfaction as it slipped away to reveal the bare posts of a bed, before landing in a crumpled pile at his feet. Kicking it impatiently to one side, he took a step forward, Isobel still pressed to his chest, and lifted them both up on to the mattress, where he immediately straddled her body with his own.

'There. Is that better?' His brows quirked with mocking amusement, settling into a dark line above eyes that glittered with both triumph and hunger. 'Is that what you meant?'

Locking his elbows, he raised his torso off hers in order to be able to look down on his captive.

'You know it isn't, Orlando.'

With her lower body pinned beneath his, Isobel raised her arms in what appeared to be an attempt to push him away. But Orlando wasn't fooled. The feeble shove against his chest was totally unconvincing and did nothing more than heighten the sexual energy between them, expose the weakening of her will. And when Orlando looked deep into her eyes he knew for certain that she was feeling it—she was feeling that raw, intimate, unspent passion every bit as much as him. No matter how much she tried to deny it. And the throbbing erection beneath his trousers, the one that was driving him crazy as it pressed forcibly against her groin, was affecting Isobel one hell of a lot more than she was prepared to say out loud.

'Tell me that you don't want this, Isobel.' Even

as he rasped the words Orlando had released one hand to undo the buckle of his belt, his fingers working the buttons of his fly.

There was a sweet silence, broken only by the soft panting of Isobel's breath.

'Tell me that you don't want me to make love to you.' Buttons undone, Orlando was now trying to tug his jeans down over his hips—frustratingly difficult with one hand.

He watched her swallow hard, her eyes darting to the exposed skin of his lower regions.

'Say the words, Isobel.'

Sitting upright now, he stifled a groan as his movement ground them together, the intimate contact shooting a bolt of pleasure right through him. He needed to rein himself in. He needed to be sure.

With a scorching glance Orlando shifted his body, lifting himself off Isobel and swinging his legs over the side of the bed—but not before he had caught the gratifying look of disappointment in her eyes. Standing tall now, he looked down on her, lying on the rumpled coverlet, watching him intently and making no attempt to escape.

He started to unbutton his shirt, his eyes never leaving hers as more and more of his broad chest was exposed until the shirt was shrugged over his shoulders and tossed to the ground. When his striptease was met with further silence he started on his jeans, pulling them lower, his boxer shorts coming down with them, until the mighty power of his erection was free from its constraints and stood hard and proud, demanding that Isobel look at it.

And look at it she did. As her eyes widened dramatically a small mew escaped her lips and she gulped, moving the pale skin of her throat.

Pulling off his jeans, Orlando threw them to one side and then straightened up to his full height, placing his hands on his hips in a shameless display of the glorious nakedness of his body.

'Come on, then, Isobel. I'm waiting.'

CHAPTER SEVEN

OH, DEAR LORD! From her supine position, Isobel stared at the glorious god of a man who stood before her, his feet firmly planted, his hands on his hips, his body gleamingly, throbbingly, totally naked.

And what a body!

All tautly gleaming muscles.

His bunched biceps rippling with barely leashed power, the sculpted pecs with their whorls of close-cropped dark hair leading the eye down to the washboard abs, the rock-hard ridges beneath olive skin shadowed darkly in the dim light.

Unable to stop herself, Isobel let her eyes travel south—how could they not? Past the jut of his hips and the indentation of his navel to where a thin line of dark hair arrowed to the star of the show—the enormous, pulsing, breathtaking erection that held itself strong and proud between Orlando's parted legs.

A gasp escaped Isobel's dry lips. What was he trying to do to her?

She blinked furiously, as if she could make Orlando vanish—take away the torment of his image. Here was the perfect specimen of man, every woman's fantasy. He was utterly irresistible. And he knew it.

Forcing herself to find the will power to drag her eyes away from this vision of virility, before the fire he had ignited deep within her core caused her to spontaneously combust, she raised her eyes to Orlando's face. Then wished she hadn't. Because the smug, satisfied, downright cocky expression she met there told her exactly what she knew already. That her pathetic protestations hadn't fooled him for one moment. That her body was betraying her in the most obvious way, from the rasping breathing that pulled her dress tight across her chest to the curl of her body as she squirmed against his imaginary touch, exposing more and more of her bare legs as the movement raised her hemline—and she was doing nothing to stop it.

It was patently obvious that she wanted him every bit as much as he wanted her. Which, judging by the size of the erection that refused to vanish from the periphery of her vision, was quite a lot.

Propping herself up on one elbow, Isobel felt her mouth fall open with longing—a longing that intensified tenfold when Orlando took a step forward so that he was only inches from her parted lips. All she would have to do was lean forward to take him, to curl her lips around the head of his member and wait for him to thrust it into her mouth in a way she knew he wouldn't be able to resist—the way he had done during one of the many times they had made love during those sultry nights on Jacamar.

God, it was tempting.

Even as she struggled to fight against the tidal wave of longing, the intense sexual need that had invaded every cell of her body, the control freak in Isobel tried to rationalise this action. If she took him in her mouth—something that was looking less and less possible to resist—it wouldn't technically count as sexual intercourse. She would be in charge. That was the important thing. She could bring him to orgasm.

Oh, God, just the thought of it made dampness pool inside her core.

She would have the all-important control. He would be the one displaying his weakness for her. Which, even though it was obviously nothing more than a carnal animal attraction, still felt pretty darned empowering right now. Yes, she would do it—make him demonstrate his need for her.

But in the feverish split-second it took her to come to this ludicrous decision everything changed. Orlando was back on the bed, straddling her, and one hand was travelling up her thigh, pushing her dress up with it. Arching over her, he dipped his head, seeking her lips, and when he found them his kiss was hot and fervent and full of a need that couldn't be tamed. A need that had Isobel totally, hopelessly and helplessly under the spell of his command. So much for that control theory.

His hand had reached her panties now, slipping under the scrap of silky fabric, his expert fingers moving unerringly to the swollen nub of her arousal, where his circling, stroking movement, together with the intense heat of his kiss, saw Isobel groan with longing, arching her back and spreading her legs as widely as the dress stretched across her thighs would allow.

The shudder of an orgasm started to build. No, this wasn't possible—not like this...not so quickly. Releasing her lips, Orlando looked down at her, revelling in his abilities, in the ease with which it happened. His gleam of triumph should have brought her to her senses, made her buck away from him and show that she was stronger than this. But with his head bent, the shadowed light accentuating the hollowed angles of his cheeks and chin, the graze of stubble across his jaw and the untamed lust darkening his eyes to black, he looked so meltingly, groaningly sexy, so utterly irresistible, that she had absolutely no chance.

'Let's get rid of these, shall we?'

Pushing himself back on his knees, he knelt before her, unceremoniously pushing up her dress so that it bunched tightly around her waist, his eagerness to get to her panties leaving no time either to remove the dress or worry about what he was doing to it. He tugged the panties down her legs with a couple of forceful yanks. When he got to her wedge-heeled sandals he hesitated for a moment before pulling them off too, tossing them over his shoulder where they fell to the floor with a thud. The panties soon joined them.

'There. That's better.'

On top of her again, he angled his naked body sideways to gain perfect access to her once more. Without the restriction of her clothes he was able to push her thighs further apart, so that his fingers could return to where they had left off, and a jolt of electrifying pleasure seared through her with their very first touch.

When he continued his unrelenting torment, increasing the pressure stroke by stroke, Isobel felt the shudder of orgasm start to build again, her body twitching, then bucking beneath his touch, an animal groan of pure pleasure blocking her throat, restricting her breathing. Then suddenly she was there—shaking, screaming out loud, wailing with the exquisite pleasure and mind-numbing release of his expertise.

As the sensation rolled over her again and again she realised that Orlando hadn't stopped. His fingers were still there, performing their magic, relentlessly prolonging the searing intensity of the sensation until she thrashed beneath him, her hair sticking to her forehead, spreading wild across the coverlet, the rapture almost too much to bear.

And then it was over. As the last violent twitches left her body she felt Orlando shift his position and, unscrewing her eyes, saw him looking down on her the way she'd known he would be, savouring her dishevelled, sweaty, totally uncontrolled wantonness. If his earlier look had been of triumph, victory, then this was one of possession—domination, even. He could do this to her—he had *done* this to her. With less than a couple of minutes of skilful lovemaking he had reduced her to the quivering mass of abandoned helplessness that he saw before him.

He had made her *his*.

As he lowered himself down onto her, Isobel closed her eyes again against the sheer thrill of his nakedness, the pressure of his erection against her groin. She felt his hair brush her chest as he dipped his head, his hand slipping the straps of her dress and bra over her shoulders to release the swell of her breasts, before his lips trailed a path of heat and damp across them that left a trail of goosebumps in their wake. And when his tongue slid into her cleavage she hooked her arms around his neck, pulling him down to increase the pressure, any vestige of self-respect gone now—it was too late. He had won.

'Tell me you want it, Isobel.' Deliberately moving so that his swollen member ground against her, Orlando searched deep into her eyes for the answer.

Too choked with desire to be able to answer, far too desperate with the yearning to feel him inside her to be able to speak, Isobel spread her legs wide, arching up in readiness for him.

'Uh-uh—not good enough, I'm afraid. I need to hear you say it.'

Why? Wasn't it all too blatantly, earth-shakingly obvious? Wasn't every fibre of her being screaming for him to take her? And yet still he held back, his body poised on the brink of penetration in a masterful display of the wretched self-control he was so proud of. Control he was now determined to parade before her to demonstrate her own total lack of it.

What was he trying to do? Make her beg?

And yet despite the almost casual demand there was no mistaking the look in his eyes—eyes that had turned liquorice black—or the slight tremble in the muscled forearms that were planted on either side of her head, the veins running in thick cords down their length.

If his pride meant that he needed her to say the words then she would say them. Because right now her need was bigger than any pride, and even though she would never get Orlando to admit it so was his.

'I want you, Orlando.' The words came out as

a husky whisper, barely escaping her lips before his mouth came down on hers for another bruising kiss.

'Say it again.' Lowering his locked elbows, he nuzzled her neck, his voice grating, his breathing ragged. 'How much do you want me, Isobel?'

'This much.' Sliding her arm down his back, she felt him twitch beneath her touch. It turned into a full spasm as she trailed her fingertips lightly over his taut buttocks, following the line of the cleft before slipping underneath him to take hold of his erection, circling its wide girth in her palm.

'*Dio*, Isobel.' He let out a long, low groan. 'That is all I need to know. Come here.'

Arching upwards, he put his hand over hers, guiding his member to Isobel's throbbing, swollen core. With the tip in place he paused, shaking with feverish desire, mirroring Isobel's own desperate longing to finish what he had started.

'I warn you…' With a deliberate movement he started to push inside, letting out a guttural groan as Isobel's clenching muscles gripped around him. 'This…is going…to be quick.'

Angling himself better, he took in a shuddering breath and then thrust, once and then again, until the whole of him was deep inside her. With a yelp of sheer delirium Isobel clung to his back, clawing her nails into his skin.

Growling an unintelligible stream of Italian

words, Orlando started to thrust, pumping with a power that had Isobel hanging on to him, each movement thrusting deeper, more forcefully than the last. As he increased speed the searing sensation became more intense, obliterating all thought in favour of pure, unadulterated sexual gratification.

As Orlando's words turned into low groans she knew that he had almost found his own release, which meant she could stop fighting the losing battle of trying to hang on to hers. With a final punishing series of deeply penetrating thrusts she felt him start to shudder, then buck, then spasm inside her. She immediately followed suit, clasping him to her, their limbs entwined as they both threw themselves headlong into the darkness of oblivion.

Minutes passed, as if time were holding its breath. With their bodies entwined and their heart rates slowing they stayed clasped together, as if pulling apart would mean facing up to the reality of what they had just done. And for Isobel that reality was the destruction of every barrier she had put in place to fend Orlando off.

The sex between had been amazing, incredible, but then it always was. The worry for Isobel was that her feelings for Orlando went way beyond the incredible sex, deeper and deeper into the fathomless depths of something far more dangerous.

Something that she was trying her hardest never to face up to.

Eventually Isobel felt Orlando shift and, loosening her grip on him, let her hand stray to the bunched-up clothes around her waist. What must she look like? She attempted to tug her dress down, rescue a bit of dignity, but it was far too late for that. Any dignity she might have had had disappeared the moment Orlando had straddled her on the bed…the moment his fingers had touched her *there*. The barriers she had been so carefully constructing to ward off his devastating power over her had come crashing down in an instant. She had wanted him so badly that she had burned with it, been flayed by it. She would have done anything, absolutely anything, to satisfy her craving need.

And would again.

Even lying there awkwardly beside him now, Isobel knew that it would only take one touch for her to be back there again. She was that weak.

'It's getting late.'

With a sudden movement Orlando pulled his body away, creating a rush of cold air that prickled across Isobel's skin, making her curl into herself. Avoiding eye contact, he swung his legs over the bed then sat with his back to Isobel, as if contemplating what the hell he had just done. A film of sweat made the muscular planes of his naked torso gleam in the dim light.

'We need to be going.'

The words were spoken harshly over his shoulder as he rose to his feet, bending to snatch up his discarded clothes from where they lay scattered on the floor. She watched his dark shape as he pulled on his boxers, closely followed by his jeans, which he tugged over his hips, slipping the belt through the heavy metal buckle with a decisive click.

She was still following his every move when he whirled round to face her, his shirt in his hands. 'Isobel?'

The sight of his dark stare brought Isobel to her senses and she scrambled off the bed, darting over to pick up the screwed up bit of fabric that was her panties and fumbling with shaky fingers to try and untwist them enough to get her legs into them. She refused to look at him as she tugged down her dress as far as it would go and cast about, searching for her handbag.

'What just happened…what we did…'

'Can I just stop you right there?' Pulling herself up to her full height, the palms of her hands held in front of her like a barrier to ward off his words, Isobel finally faced him. 'If you are going to say that it shouldn't have happened, then please don't bother. I already know that.'

'I wasn't, actually.' Orlando's voice was flat, devoid of all emotion.

'Well, don't tell me that you're sorry either.' Isobel rearranged her hair, combing it through with her fingers. 'Because that would be even worse.'

'What *is* it with you, Isobel?' Shrugging on his shirt now, Orlando started to do up the buttons with unnecessary force, his eyes never leaving her face. 'Standing there, telling me what I am thinking, what I am going to say, like you know me better than I know myself...'

Staring at the towering silhouette that smouldered before her, Isobel dragged in a breath. 'I am just trying to make you see that you don't need to justify or apologise for what we did. That's all.'

'I can assure you I have no intention of doing any such thing.'

Taking a single step towards her, Orlando reached forward to frame her face in his hands, tilting it towards the last of the dying light from the window in order to be able to see her better.

'I just wanted to make sure that you were all right. *That's all.*'

'I am absolutely fine.' Isobel felt her jaw move against his warm hands, his breath fanning her face. 'As you can see.'

'And the baby?' Orlando paused, his voice suddenly gruff as his eyes searched her face and he struggled to find the right words. 'I wasn't too rough?'

So that was it. Orlando wasn't worried about *her*, or the fact that what they had just done had opened up the floodgates of forbidden feelings—for her, at least. He was just thinking about the baby.

Reclaiming her face with a toss of her head, she fought to heal the crack in her voice. 'Rest assured, the baby and I are both fine.'

'*Bene*. Good.' Conscience clear, Orlando moved away and started to cross the room, stopping in the doorway to wait for Isobel to join him. 'You are ready to leave now?'

'Yes.' Turning to look back one last time at the rumpled bed, at the dust sheet on the floor beside it, Isobel drew in a painful breath and hurried towards him, suddenly desperate to get away. 'Let's go.'

CHAPTER EIGHT

UP, DRESSED AND with her bag packed, Isobel was ready to leave by first light.

On their return to the hotel the night before, Orlando had briskly informed her that they would be leaving the following morning, his private plane taking them both back to London and then him on to New York. Seating himself at his laptop, he had then pointedly immersed himself in work, leaving no room for further conversation. Not that Isobel had wanted any. She'd just wanted to put as much distance between them as fast as possible, although she suspected even an ocean apart wouldn't be enough.

Taking herself off to bed, she had hoped for the oblivion of sleep but it hadn't happened. Instead she had found herself staring up at the ceiling, thinking about the baby and about Orlando, trying to come to terms with everything that had happened to her within a few short weeks.

To her surprise, the baby was already a source of great joy. The tiny scrap of life growing inside her which had caused so much trouble, turned her life upside down, was already loved with all her heart. She had never imagined herself as a mother, somehow convinced that she wouldn't have the necessary qualifications—whatever they were. After all, she had failed dismally as a daughter, something her own mother managed to enforce tacitly every time they met.

But now that the completely unexpected had happened she had been surprised to discover a new-found confidence. She was going to be a *good* mother. The responsibility didn't frighten her— she had been coping with responsibility ever since her father had died. And she had plenty of love to give…bucketloads of it…already spilling over when she thought of holding the child in her arms. What *did* scare her was Orlando, and the fact that he was so determined to play a large part in their baby's life. Which would mean a large part of *her* life. Something that managed to astonish, terrify and secretly thrill her in equal measure.

Inevitably, the sleepless hours had seen her torturing herself with what they had done the evening before. She was furious with herself for letting it happen, and yet couldn't stop thinking about it, replaying what they had done until it had driven her half crazy.

The memory of the expert skill of his lovemaking, the exquisite sensations he had aroused, had sent spasms of awareness through her sleepless body that had seen her clenching her thighs to stop their progress, had made her sit up and grope for the glass of water on the bedside table to try to douse the spreading ache. It was madness—she knew that. But it was a madness she could no longer control.

As the hours of darkness had crept on, so had the cold certainty that as far as Orlando Cassano was concerned, she was way out of her depth. In fact, she was drowning.

By the time dawn had started to fan its light across the ceiling, Isobel had been forced to face up to the terrible truth. The truth she had been trying so hard to ignore ever since that fateful moment when she had taken his hand and stepped off the boat on to the island of Jacamar.

She had fallen in love with Orlando Cassano. Senselessly, crazily, idiotically in love. And right now that felt like the most disastrous thing in the world.

Because she knew that her love would never be reciprocated—knew that Orlando would never, *could* never return the plunging depths of the feelings she had for him. For Orlando had shown her what lay beneath the charming, urbane exterior. He had exposed the man who lay within. Heartless, cold-blooded and ruthless. A man who intended to erase his past as if it had never existed. Who had displayed a chilling lack of emotion when it came to the child she was carrying other than to ensure that he had full control. And who showed no feelings for her—unless you counted irritation, of course, or frustration, or lust. Oh, yes, he felt that last one, all right, no matter how much he tried to fight it. But that was no comfort to Isobel. It just twisted the knife still further.

Their suite of rooms was empty when Isobel emerged from her bedroom. The door to Orlando's room was open but the room was obviously unoccupied. Sliding the heavy doors across, Isobel went out onto the balcony, then hesitated. The glass floor, which no doubt had looked great on the designer's plans, was doing absolutely nothing to help her morning sickness. The scarily clear view of the waves crashing on the rocks below flipped her stomach like a pancake.

Telling herself not to be such a baby, she shuffled her way to the edge and, leaning on the steel handrail, took in the scene before her. The Adriatic Sea twinkled in the early-morning sun, stretching to the horizon where it met the milky blue sky. Boats of different shapes and sizes bobbed on the water and seagulls wheeled overhead, their cries carried by the breeze.

'Buongiorno.'

Spinning around too suddenly, Isobel had to stretch out her arms on either side to grasp the railings, her grip tightening further at the sight of Orlando standing in the doorway. Wearing a black vest that perspiration had moulded against his torso, and jogging bottoms low on his hips, he

was all rippling biceps and unkempt tousled hair.
And raw sex appeal.

'Good morning.' Isobel swallowed. 'You've been
for a run.' There was nothing like stating the obvious.

'*Sì.*' Taking a swig from the water bottle in his
hand, Orlando stared at her. 'I had some excess energy to burn off.' The stare intensified. 'You okay?'

'Yes.' Isobel almost hissed the word. Why did he
persist in asking how she was? Especially in a way
that suggested he should be able to control that too?

'I'm going to take a shower.' He turned and
headed inside, calling over his shoulder, 'If you
want to order breakfast I'll be with you in ten minutes.'

The waiters had just finished laying out the
breakfast when Orlando re-emerged. Isobel caught
the citrus-sharp tang of his aftershave as he moved
behind her to take his seat opposite. Wearing dark
jeans and a white shirt, sleeves rolled up to the elbows, he appeared composed, coolly distant.

'You didn't want to eat on the balcony?' Shaking open his napkin, Orlando reached for the coffee pot.

'Um…no.' Not if she wanted to stand any chance
of keeping any food down, she didn't. Isobel had
asked for their breakfast to be served on the dining
table inside—a polished slab of limestone, complete with fossils. 'It was too bright for me.'

Orlando briefly narrowed his gaze before helping himself to a healthy portion of muesli and topping it with fresh fruit.

'What time is our flight back this morning?' Taking a sip of peppermint tea, Isobel surveyed her bowl of fruit, wondering if she was brave enough to take a mouthful.

'There's been a change of plan.' Orlando looked up briefly. 'I've booked an evening flight now.'

'Oh.' Isobel watched as he returned to his breakfast rather than offering her any sort of explanation. But she wasn't going to make a fuss, telling herself it was only a few more hours. She could be cool with that.

'Orlando, about yesterday…'

Argh, yesterday—why was she talking about yesterday? Because it was all she could think about, that was why. And because something about Orlando's hurtful detachment, his unspoken denial, made her want to make him face up to what they had done. Even though she didn't want to face up to it herself.

'Yesterday?'

'Yes.' It was too late to back down now. 'I need to make it clear that it won't happen again.'

'Right.'

She had his full attention now, and the dark glitter of his eyes was replaying what they had done as clearly as if he were speaking the words.

'And you are sure about that, are you?'

'Quite sure. From now on I think it's important that we conduct our relationship in a businesslike manner.'

'Do you, now?'

'Yes—yes, I do. I've been working it out. All being well, if the business forecast is correct and the sales in the new stores go well, I predict that I should be able to exercise my right to buy back the twenty per cent of shares from Cassano Holdings to give me a majority shareholding in Spicer Shoes in approximately twelve months—eighteen at the latest.'

'And the baby, Isobel?' Orlando's withering reply whistled through the air. 'Are you planning on trying to buy back my fifty per cent of that too?'

'Don't be ridiculous.' Isobel put down her spoon to stare at the dark head opposite her, at the thick, damp hair curling as it dried.

She knew what she was trying to do. She was focussing on the one thing she thought she had some hope of controlling: her business. Figuring out when she would be free of Orlando's overbearing authority in that department was all she had to cling to at the moment.

But as for the baby… She had no idea how that was going to work out. But one thing she did know. As far as Orlando was concerned their baby was non-negotiable. And that worry sat like a lead yoke around her shoulders.

'With the baby we are just going to have to do the best we can. Find some sort of arrangement that is mutually agreeable.'

'Ah, yes, a *mutually agreeable* arrangement. I'm glad you've said that, Isobel, because I think I have come up with just the thing.'

The unsettling gleam in Orlando's dark eyes shot a spark of alarm through Isobel.

'Go on.'

'Castello Trevente, the Trevente estate, I've decided not to sell it.'

'You have?' Isobel's eyebrows arched high with surprise. 'Well, I'm very pleased that you have seen sense.'

'I thought you would be.'

If this was a victory, something about Orlando's overly relaxed attitude was making her far too nervous to enjoy it.

'Can I ask what made you change your mind?'

'You did, Isobel.' Reaching for the coffee pot again, Orlando refilled his cup and raised it to his lips. 'You made me realise that this legacy is not mine to ignore or sell, that we have our child to think about now—the future Marchese di Trevente. To deny him his birthright would be quite wrong.'

'I don't think I actually said that.' Isobel could feel the fingers of panic running along her spine as she started to see where this was going. When she had fought so hard to save the *castello* she hadn't meant to use their unborn child as hostage. 'I'm glad that you have decided not to forgo your inheritance, Orlando, I'm sure it's the right decision.' Tiptoeing through the minefield, she hesitated. 'But I think it is a little early to start mapping out the future for our child.'

'On the contrary. I have given it a lot of thought and this is the obvious solution.' He fixed her with his most imperious stare. 'Castello Trevente will be our family home.'

Orlando leant back, enjoying watching Isobel assimilate this information. He noticed the way her teeth nipped at the soft pout of her bottom lip. Her hands fluttered to her throat, and pink circles of colour stained her cheeks.

Get out of this one, Miss Spicer. He allowed himself a secret smile. Because he was ready for her. Isobel never did anything she was told, never accepted anything without a fight—especially where he was concerned. But this was a fight he was going to win. He needed to claw back some control after what had happened yesterday.

He still wasn't sure how they had ended up in bed. The rage he had felt when Isobel had challenged him, standing there spouting her amateur psychology, had certainly brought a red mist to his eyes. But somehow that anger had turned into a carnal craving that had resulted in the most astounding sex he could ever remember. Did he regret it? No. Even if Isobel obviously did, with her prickly manner and her little *'conduct our relationship in a businesslike manner'* speech. Well, they would see about that. Frankly, business was the last thing on his mind as far as Isobel Spicer was concerned.

Orlando had spent the intervening hours taking a long, hard look at the situation, trying to see past the complicated mix of emotions to find a solution. He'd taken himself off for a long, punishing run and the answer had finally come to him.

If Isobel was so keen on preserving the *castello*, then clearly this was where they should live. Where their child should be raised. He would be acknowledging that he had listened to her concerns at the same time as demonstrating that he was prepared to adapt his life for his child in the same way he expected *her* to. And, of course, he would be protecting their child's heritage. Something he had to admit he hadn't even considered until Isobel had taken it upon herself to point it out.

He would accept the title of Marchese di Trevente, restore the *castello* to its former glory and get the estate back on its feet. Something he would never have imagined doing in his wildest dreams. But then neither had he ever imagined being a father. And, stranger still, the more he got used to the idea, the more surprised he was to find that he liked it.

But moving back to Trevente would mean facing the demons of his past. Sophia's death had shaped his whole existence and it would stay with him for ever. Nothing would ever ease the guilt he felt, the clawing reality that she had died because of *him*—that he could have prevented her death if only he had stopped his father that night...if only he hadn't made the warehouse their meeting place...if only they had never fallen in love.

But if he had to struggle with the battleground of his past in order to secure a future for himself and his child, then he would do it. And maybe it wouldn't be all bad. The thought of living with Isobel gave him a sort of masochistic pleasure, pumped adrenaline through his body, like walking over hot coals or leaping off a cliff. And then, of course, there was the sex... Mind-blowing it might be, but sex was all it could ever be. He had to make sure of that. For Isobel's own sake he would protect her from his dark heart. From a heart that had shrivelled in the fire all those years ago as surely as if it too had died in the flames.

'You are suggesting that I move to Italy?' The words came out in a quiet trickle of anxiety. 'That we live in Castello Trevente together?'

'*Sì.*'

A frown creased Isobel's brow, marring her

beautiful face. He could almost see the cogs of her mind whirring, trying to find a way out.

'It's the obvious solution as you appear to be so enamoured of the place.' His lips flattened with the distaste he knew that he had to control. 'London is no more than two hours away. We'll put a manager in the workshop and I will ensure that a private jet is available to you at all times. Plus there will be definite advantages to being close to the factory.'

Isobel shook her head. 'I can't, Orlando. I can't leave the UK.' She chewed nervously at her bottom lip. 'There's something, or rather someone, I haven't mentioned to you before.'

Immediately an iron fist gripped his guts. *He knew it. There was someone else.*

'Go on.' He heard himself grate the words.

'My mother.' Isobel sucked in a breath.

'Your *mother*?' The iron grip loosened and relief washed over him—an alien sensation swiftly replaced by more familiar irritation. What did her mother have to do with anything? Isobel was really scraping the bottom of the barrel now.

'Yes. She lives in a residential home on the outskirts of London.'

'And your point is…?'

'She's not well, Orlando. She needs me. I can't move to a different country and leave her on her own.'

'Then hire a nurse—or bring her with you for

all I care.' His patience was starting to wear decidedly thin now.

He could see the fleeting look of pain that crossed Isobel's face and was surprised by the resulting kick he felt in his gut. Was the idea of living with him so abhorrent to her? He wasn't enjoying this as much as he'd thought.

'But how could we live in the *castello*? You said yourself it's in a terrible state. It's not a fit place for a newborn baby. It will be winter by then and...'

'Give me *some* credit, Isobel. Castello Trevente will be completely renovated. In fact I have set up a meeting with some architects for this afternoon.'

'This afternoon?'

'*Sì*. They are flying over from New York as we speak.' Orlando watched her swallow back her surprise. 'We are meeting them at the *castello* at three p.m. That's why we're taking a later flight back to the UK.'

From her silence Orlando could see that he had worn her down—that he was winning. He let his gaze linger on her face as he waited with interest to see what she was going to come up with next, almost looking forward to it. Because whatever it was it would make no difference. He would have the answer. He wasn't going to let her slip through the net this time.

But when Isobel finally spoke she took him by surprise.

Pulling her composure back into place she coolly met his gaze. 'Very well.' She sat up straight. 'If you are sure that this is the best solution, then I agree. I will move into Castello Trevente with you.'

Orlando stared at her. Had he heard her right? Was she actually agreeing to his proposition? He knew he had to find his own composure quickly, before she changed her mind.

'Bene.' Careful to keep the surprise out of his voice, Orlando returned to his breakfast. 'I am so glad we have sorted that out.'

'Great. Well, I think we are nearly done here.' Luke, one of the team of six architects, looked up from the plans that littered the table. 'We just need to decide where you want the nursery.'

Stupidly, Isobel felt herself blush. So Orlando had told them, then—this vibrant young team he'd had flown over from New York, who were now seated at the enormous scrubbed table in the basement kitchen. Why did that feel so weird?

Because Isobel realised that *she* had told no one—not even her mother. Because telling people would make it feel frighteningly real.

She looked around the table at the shiny bright faces of these enthusiastic people. They seemed so cheerful, so *untroubled*, that for a moment she longed to swap places with one of them, to forget about the horribly tortured, complicated life she suddenly found herself in and be optimistic and carefree like them.

It was something she realised she had never been—at least not since the age of seventeen, when the car crash had decimated her family and left her weighed down with grief, responsibility and an overriding sense of guilt.

'We thought maybe this room.' An extremely attractive blonde called Millie pointed a manicured finger at the plans. 'Next to the master bedroom. But maybe you would rather locate it up on the next floor? Perhaps a suite of rooms, to accommodate a nanny?'

'No.' Isobel's sharp reply made Millie raise her clear blue eyes in surprise. 'I mean… I don't know if we will be having a nanny.'

Isobel shot a glance at Orlando, wanting him to make these questions go away. In reply he gave a small dismissive shrug. He was being no help at all—in fact he had given very little input to the whole restoration project, either deferring to Isobel or giving the architects a free hand. A gymnasium and a swimming pool had been his only two requirements.

'The room next to the master bedroom will be fine.'

'Fantastic.' Millie's clever eyes had followed hers and they now swept across Orlando, pausing for a split second to take in the scene. 'Can I just say thank you again for choosing us for this project? We are always thrilled to work on any of your assignments, Orlando, but this is a dream of a job.'

This was greeted with agreement all round, but Isobel couldn't help looking at the way Millie was flicking her shiny hair over her shoulder, crossing one shapely leg over the other. If she wasn't mistaken, now she was actually licking her lips.

A dart of jealousy shot through her, even as she told herself that she was being ridiculous, that this young woman was simply showing her appreciation for being given such a prestigious job. But still she couldn't banish the image of other ways Millie might like to show her appreciation—especially as Orlando was doing nothing to discourage her attention, reciprocating with a small smile and the quirk of a brow that epitomised his infuriating easy charm... That was guaranteed to send any woman running for his bedroom.

Suddenly she needed to get away. 'Well...' She rose to her feet. 'If that's it for today, I think I need to stretch my legs.'

'Yes, of course.'

Following her cue, everyone stood up and after offering her thanks and shaking a lot of hands Isobel was finally able to make her escape, her forced smile only chilling slightly as it swept over the twinkling Millie.

Alone at last, Isobel stretched her cramped

limbs. They had been sitting around that table for hours, but they had certainly achieved a lot. After a whirlwind tour the team had worked like demons to gather information, checking that they fully understood the brief with every clever idea they came up with. There was no doubt that Castello Trevente was going to be completely stunning by the time they had finished with it. Even if it did still seem incredible to Isobel that she would be the one actually living here.

She knew she had surprised Orlando earlier, when she had agreed to his idea without putting up much of a fight. But they were going to have to live together somewhere—and he was offering her a *castle*, for heaven's sake. And there was another reason too—one she hadn't bothered to share with him. Her mother, Nancy. Isobel didn't know if Orlando had meant it when he had so dismissively stated that she could come and live with them, but it had set her thinking.

It was a good idea. Better than that—it was an excellent idea.

She had long suspected that being closeted in that nursing home wasn't doing her mother any good. Isobel hated the place. Her dutiful twice weekly visits were always guaranteed to induce a sick feeling in her stomach; the overheated temperature, the particular smell—a mixture of antiseptic and lilies—and the soulless greetings of the overworked staff all served as a constant reminder of the blighted life that her mother now led because of the accident...because of *her*.

She dreaded sitting on the chair opposite her mother, watching her bird-like frame getting more frail with every passing year, listening to the growing list of ailments and grievances that Isobel could do nothing about. Except to be there for her. Because despite her mother's cold disregard they both knew that Isobel was all Nancy Spicer had. They were in this together. For ever.

Which was why having her mother move to Italy with her made perfect sense. Not only would Isobel be close at hand at all times, but the Italian climate would surely be beneficial for her.

Isobel made up her mind to put the idea to her as soon she returned to the UK, to try and phrase it in such a way that her mother couldn't say no. And she would finally tell her about the baby too...a conversation that was well overdue.

Now she wandered out into the hallway, deciding to take a last look around in order to remember the place in all its faded grandeur. Climbing the stairs, she found herself drawn to the bedroom where she and Orlando had committed that act of madness the night before.

Earlier, when they had walked into that room with the architects, her heart had been thumping, her eyes darting madly from Orlando to the rumpled silk coverlet on the bed and back again. She had been convinced that the evidence of what they had done had to be visible, that the intense heat of their sexual encounter must have scorched their images on the silk. But Orlando hadn't acknowledged her gaze, showing no outward sign that this room, or the bed, or indeed Isobel herself had any particular significance. Instead he had strolled around, pointing out the crumbling cornice, kicking at the rotten skirting board, before marching out again with the architects' team tagging behind like devoted followers.

Now Isobel bent to retrieve the dust cover that was still lying on the floor. Picking it up, she shook it high in the air and watched it settle over the bed, walking round to straighten the corners as if she could somehow cover up what they had done. But it was far too late for that. There was no covering up the reality of her life from now on. She would be living in a castle, with Orlando, and bearing him a child. Those were the facts she had to deal with, and that was what she had to concentrate on. Because facing up to anything else was too painful, too raw. All she could do was try to contain her emotions and protect herself from the intensity of her feelings for Orlando as best she could. If she could keep her heart locked away, maybe he wouldn't find it.

She climbed the winding stairs to the medieval

tower that had enchanted the architects so much. The oldest part of the *castello*, it had a low arched doorway that opened out on to the battlements with their crumbling stonework. Orlando had shown no inclination to go out there, but now Isobel turned the key in the lock and stepped outside. The crenulated wall was about waist-high at its lowest point, rising to eye level, and the gaps between afforded the most stunning views: the mountains in one direction, the sea in the other, with villages, rolling green fields and the town of Trevente spread out like a colourful tapestry.

Being careful not to touch the stonework, Isobel paced the circuit to take in the views from every angle, stopping only when she reached the front of the *castello* and saw that the team of architects was leaving.

She watched as Orlando walked down the driveway with them towards their minivan, where the driver was already opening the doors. After shaking hands with the men, he kissed the two women on the cheek. Isobel saw the way Millie leant in, standing on tiptoe to reach him better, placing her hands possessively on his shoulders.

She scowled, turning away to go back downstairs. She had enough problems without torturing herself with jealousy over every attractive woman who happened to cross Orlando's path. Because, frankly, if she did that the men in white coats would be carting her away before this baby was even born. In fact, the way she felt right now that was looking like a distinct possibility.

She was back down in the hallway just as Orlando walked in.

'Are you ready to go?'

Isobel nodded, then felt her heart still as Orlando slipped his hand around her waist to usher her out into the evening sunshine. Locking the door behind them, he slipped the key into his pocket.

'I imagine it will look very different the next time we see it.' Determined to be positive, Isobel stepped back and looked up at the old building.

'I very much hope so.' Orlando didn't follow her gaze, instead heading down the path towards the car with long strides. It seemed he couldn't get away fast enough.

CHAPTER NINE

OPENING HER EMAILS, Isobel saw the message from Orlando and her heart immediately started to thud. He'd been in contact several times over the six weeks they had been apart—her in London, him in New York—but that didn't stop the visceral reaction every time she saw his name, even if the message was only to discuss something to do with the business or to update her on the restoration of the *castello*, or maybe check that she was attending her doctor's appointments in his usual controlling way.

The dates of her pregnancy had been confirmed now, and all was looking just as it should. Isobel had had an ultrasound scan, and the amazing, grainy black-and-white image of their tiny baby was propped up on her mantelpiece at home, where she gazed at it in awe every time she passed.

Sadly, breaking the news of the pregnancy to her mother had been just as negative an experience as Isobel had anticipated. Nancy Spicer had met Isobel's nervous disclosure with distaste, only showing a flicker of interest when Isobel had told her that the baby's father held the title of Marchese di Trevente, and that he was in fact a very wealthy man. Pouncing on this one glimmer of curiosity, Isobel had rushed straight on, announcing that she would be moving to Italy, and that Nancy was very welcome to come and live with them at the *castello*—indeed, that she very much hoped she would.

Her mother's instinctive reaction had been to say that it was the most ridiculous idea she had ever heard—that Isobel should go, run away, leave her mother to her sad and lonely life the way she knew she had always wanted to. But the vulnerable look in her eyes had told a different story, and Isobel was confident that eventually her mother would come round to the idea. First, though, she would have to convince herself and everyone else that she was only doing it for her daughter, because Isobel had begged her.

So, with those delicate negotiations underway, Isobel had used the rest of the six weeks to throw herself wholeheartedly into her work. It was as good a distraction as any, and there had certainly been plenty to do. Work on the two new stores in London and New York was progressing well, and they were on schedule to open in the autumn as planned. The factory in Trevente was running smoothly, Spicer shoes were now selling in prestigious department stores across the world—not just London, as before—and new orders were flooding in all the time.

Now, as she sat in her office, Isobel could hear

the reassuring tap-tap of hammers coming from the workshop next door, where the master shoe-makers were chattering over the sound of the radio as they worked. This was where Isobel felt safe, grounded: at the heart of the Spicer Shoes business. This was where her designs were brought to life before hitting the production line, where the handmade shoes were still created. And even though that market was tiny, compared to the global juggernaut of mass production that she and Orlando had put in place, it was still the part of the business that Isobel loved the best. And the one she would be leaving behind when she went to live in Italy.

The wrench would be enormous. She knew that. Not only would she be removing herself from the cosy hub of the Spicer Shoes empire, but also saying goodbye to London, to her apartment and her friends, to the network she had built up over the years. Everything that she had ever known. But needs must. Or, as her mother had so tersely put it, *'You've made your bed, young lady, you must lie in it.'*

The very thing that, thinking about it, had got her into this mess in the first place.

Clicking on the email, Isobel felt her heart spike wildly.

Castello Trevente is finished.

She read Orlando's words again. So it had really happened. Despite the updates she'd been receiving from the architects, and Orlando's calm assurances that the timescale would be met, she hadn't really believed that it was possible to renovate a whole castle in six weeks. But this was the power of Orlando. He literally made things happen.

I suggest we meet there on Friday.
Orlando.

Isobel swallowed the lump of alarm in her throat. Friday? *This* Friday?

With her fingers on the keyboard she started to type her reply, rapidly telling him she couldn't possibly be ready by Friday, that there was no way she could have everything in place and be able to move by then.

But halfway through her frantic rant she stopped. What was the point? It was only postponing the inevitable. Wouldn't it be better to face her fate full-on? Show Orlando that she was calm, capable, in control? Far better than scurrying around making excuses.

Pressing the backspace button, she watched the letters on the screen disappear and then, taking in a deep breath, she began again.

Friday will be fine, Orlando.

Ignoring the panic in her heart, she carried on.

I will see you then.

Walking into Castello Trevente, Isobel caught her breath—it had been transformed! Gone was the peeling paintwork in the hallway, the rotten panelling and the smell of damp. Now the marble staircase gleamed, and sweeping wrought-iron banisters drew the eye up to the restored cupola several flights above. Exotic flower arrangements scented the air, a splash of colour against the immaculate powder-blue walls.

A small cough beside her told Isobel she wasn't alone and, turning, she saw the smiling face of a middle-aged woman, her arm outstretched in greeting.

'Signorina Spicer?'

'Yes—*sì*. That's right.'

'I am very glad to meet you. My name is Maria Marelli and I am your housekeeper.'

'Hello, Maria.' Shaking her hand, Isobel smiled back warmly, instantly liking this cheerful woman. 'And, please, you must call me Isobel.'

'*Sì, certo.* So, Isobella…' Standing back, Maria gestured around her before placing her hands on her not-inconsiderable hips. 'You like?'

'I *do* like!' Isobel looked around her in disbelief. 'It's stunning! I can't wait to see the rest of the *castello*.'

'Everywhere is *bello—molto bello*. I tell you, it is unbelievable. I want to thank you—you and the Marchese—for doing this…for bringing Castello Trevente back to life. And to think you will live here, raise a family here.' Maria clasped her hands together and raised her eyes heavenwards. 'It is a dream for us—for all the people who work on the estate. A dream we never thought would come true.'

Suddenly uncomfortable, Isobel moved her hands automatically to cover her stomach, even though at a little over three months pregnant she was only showing the slightest of bumps. She couldn't take Maria's gratitude; it made her feel like a fraud. Because the genuine warmth and excitement she obviously felt for the new incumbents of Castello Trevente was sadly misplaced. Isobel and Orlando would never be able to give this place the fairy tale it deserved.

'Orlando—the Marchese, I mean…' Isobel had no idea how he would want Maria to address him. 'He hasn't arrived yet?'

'No.' Maria shook her head. 'He is late already. But you are here at least. You must be tired and hungry after your journey. You would like to go into the drawing room and I bring you something to eat?'

'I'm fine, thank you, Maria. Though a cup of tea would be nice.'

'Very good. I bring you English tea.' Turning on her heel, Maria hurried off towards the kitchens. 'The Marchese—he say it must be English tea.'

Sipping her English tea in the drawing room, Isobel looked around her, amazed at the transformation. It was hard to believe that this was the same room she and Orlando had been standing in the last time she had visited the *castello*, only a few short weeks ago. The furniture had been restored; the sofas regilded and reupholstered, the carpets repaired, and the ancestral portraits had been given a new lease of life and returned to the walls, from where they looked down on her with mild disapproval.

Having finished her tea, Isobel saw there was still no sign of Orlando so set off to explore the rest of the *castello*. Maria was right. It *was 'molto bello'*. The care and attention to detail and the sheer skill of the architects and builders was evident everywhere she looked.

Walking into the room that was now the nursery, Isobel was suddenly pulled up short. With pale yellow walls and white paintwork it looked fresh and sunny, but it was the crib in the centre of the room that made her heart flutter like the beat of a bird's wing. Carved from dark wood, and festooned with soft cotton drapes, it was obviously an antique—a family heirloom. Moving forward to inspect it, Isobel felt it rock silently beneath her touch, and the sudden image of her baby sleeping there both astonished and thrilled her. She *had* to get used to the idea that this really was happening.

But where was Orlando? The longer Isobel waited for him to arrive, the more her anxiety levels rose.

She had been bracing herself for this meeting all week, trying to prepare herself for the onslaught of emotions that she knew seeing Orlando again would unleash. For the six weeks they had been apart he had been constantly in her thoughts, especially at night, when he'd filled her head, twisting her heart with a longing so intense that she had thought she might burn with it.

But she was a sensible girl. She knew the score. She knew she had to banish any silly fantasies of happy-ever-after and accept Orlando for who he was. She could never make him love her. She doubted anyone could.

As the hours passed her nervousness increased, and by the time Maria served her a light supper in the echoing dining room Isobel wasn't able to eat a thing.

By eleven o'clock, when Orlando had still not shown, her anxiety levels had gone through the roof—spreading from nervousness to outrage to a barely controlled fury that he had the audacity to keep her waiting like this. After all, this had all been his idea. And now, on their first night in the *castello*, he hadn't even had the courtesy to turn up.

Finally, having run the exhausting gamut of emotions, Isobel settled on the most depressing idea of all. Orlando wasn't coming. He had changed his mind. He had obviously realised that tying himself down to her and the baby was a sacrifice he was no longer prepared to make.

Rising stiffly from the antique sofa where she had been perched, frozen, for the last hour, Isobel held on to the back to steady herself. Tomorrow she would go back to England, put all this behind her, and concentrate on making the life for herself and her baby that she had intended to make from the start—before Orlando had crashed in with his demands and ultimatums.

She had got as far as the doorway when she heard a commotion on the other side. Flinging open the door, she saw Maria, ashen-faced, her shaking hands at her mouth, and behind her a middle-aged man wearing a full-length nightshirt, attempting to console her.

'Maria?'

'Oh, Isobella!' At the sight of Isobel fat tears started to stream down her face.

'Maria, what is it?'

'It is the Marchese.' A sob escaped her chest and Isobel had to wait for an agonising second for it to subside, fear gripping at her heart.

'Orlando?'

'*Sì*, Orlando. He has been in a terrible accident.'

Running down the hospital corridor, with the young doctor trying to keep up with her, Isobel desperately tried to take in the information he was giving her. But panic had set in, making the blood roar in her ears, shutting out all reason and feeling apart from the overwhelmingly urgent need to see Orlando for herself. As if she alone was the one person who could make him better.

He had been in a car accident and he was in hospital. That much Isobel had gleaned from Maria before a wave of sickness had washed over her and she had collapsed to the ground in a dead faint. She had woken, seconds later, shivering violently against the marble tiles, to hear Maria wailing and to feel the poor unknown man struggling to get her into sitting position.

Even through the daze of nausea it had been clear to her that she was going to have to take charge if she wanted to see Orlando straight away. So she had pulled herself up to stand, gripping the walls for support, and announced to the distraught couple that she had to get to the hospital, that she needed a taxi, or a driver, or a car that she could drive herself if necessary. In the end it had been the man, Pietro, who'd turned out to be Maria's husband, who had come to her rescue, running to put on some clothes before bringing a car around to the front, whilst Maria had fussed over Isobel, insisting she took sips of water and arranging a blanket over her shoulders.

Now, as Isobel and the doctor stopped outside the door to what must be Orlando's room, she could feel that wave of sickness threatening to engulf her again. She took in a shuddering breath.

'Signor Cassano has received a significant head injury…'

She heard the doctor trying to prepare her but his well-meaning words only terrified her more.

'He will be drowsy and may appear confused. This will be the result of the medication and not necessarily the result of any brain damage.'

'Brain damage?' The words lodged like ice in her throat.

'The X-rays and scans have not revealed anything untoward, but we have no way of knowing how long Signor Cassano was unconscious. With head injuries, sometimes the damage does not show immediately. He will need to be closely monitored for the next twenty-four hours before we will be able to rule out the possibility completely.'

'I understand.' Isobel managed a small nod. 'Please, can I see him now?'

Opening the door, the doctor ushered her in, following close behind.

Orlando was lying in bed, propped up by pillows, his eyes firmly closed. Even here, under the harsh hospital lights he managed to look magnificent, commanding, as if he owned the place.

Bare-chested, at first sight he appeared unscathed, with just a blood-pressure cuff and a wire leading from the patch below his collarbone to link him to the humming machines. But as Isobel went to stand beside him she could see the egg-shaped swelling on the side of his forehead, the skin there already starting to take on the colour of what was going to be an almighty bruise.

She leant over him, kissing him lightly on his brow that was furrowed, even in sleep. As her hair brushed against his face she saw him twitch, his eyes flickering beneath the closed lids.

Sitting down, she looked at the injury more closely, her fingers itching to touch it, to run over the swelling as if she could heal it. But instead she took hold of Orlando's hand in hers, surprised to feel a quick, but very firm grip in response.

'He is obviously sleeping now, which is good.' The doctor smiled at Isobel. 'If you want to leave and come back in the morning? We will of course let you know should there be any change in his condition.'

Isobel felt Orlando's grip tighten again.

'Thank you, but I would like to stay.'

'Of course. Then I will leave you alone. Please press the buzzer if you require anything or have any concerns.'

'Thank you, I will.'

As the door clicked softly behind the doctor Isobel turned back to Orlando, just in time to see one eye open, then the other.

'Isobel. *Meno male*—thank God. Pass me my clothes.'

'What?' Releasing his hand, Isobel shot back.

'I said pass me my clothes. We are leaving.'

'What are you talking about, Orlando? The doctor has just told me…'

'I don't care what he told you. It's just a bump on the head. We are out of here—now.'

Isobel watched in horror as Orlando swung his legs over the bed, pulling off the wires and reaching for the clothes that were neatly folded on a chair.

'How did you get here? By taxi?'

'No, Pietro brought me.'

'Is he still here?' He was pulling on his jeans now, buttoning the fly.

'Yes.' She had left Pietro waiting outside in the car.

'*Eccellente*. We just need to slip out without being noticed.'

'We will do no such thing.' Leaping to her feet,

Isobel made for the buzzer above the bed. 'If you don't get back into bed I am going to press this buzzer and get help.'

'And if *you* don't step away from the buzzer I won't be responsible for my actions.'

They faced each other from either side of the bed, eyes flashing. Outrage at Orlando's plan was making the breath heave in Isobel's chest. He *couldn't* just walk out—not after what the doctor had told her.

'Come on, Isobel.' Orlando stretched out his arms wide. 'See for yourself. There is nothing wrong with me.'

Isobel blinked, determined not to be swayed by his blatant display of masculinity. 'And that huge swelling on your head is "nothing", is it?'

'Just a bump.' Raising his hand, Orlando touched the injury, suppressing a sharp wince. 'That's all.'

'You need to be monitored for twenty-four hours, Orlando. That's what the doctor said.'

'Fine.'

As he pulled his shirt over his head Isobel saw him grimace again, and when he bent to tug on his boots, stuffing his socks into his pockets, it was obvious that he was in a lot more pain than he was ever going to admit.

'I hereby appoint you my chief monitor. Now, let's go.'

'You can't do this, Orlando.'

But Orlando had already reached the door and, opening it quietly, he lowered his voice to a harsh whisper. 'Here's the deal, Isobel.' He shot her a piercing stare. 'Either you agree to watch over me or I take my chances and hope for the best. The choice is yours.'

Shifting his position slightly, Orlando tentatively moved his legs across the bed, then pushed his shoulders back into the mattress to try and relieve the stiffness.

'Are you okay? Do you need another pillow?'

'No, I'm fine.'

'Fine' didn't exactly sum up how he felt. Although determined not to show it, Orlando was feeling pretty murderous. This was *not* how he had intended to spend his first night in the master bedroom of the *castello*. Quite apart from the thumping headache and the aching bones, he was furious to find himself in this position of weakness. Furious with himself for driving too fast, furious with the wretched stag that had bounded across his path, and with the gods that had seen fit to bring the two elements together.

The violent impact had been enough to see him career off the road and into a ditch, banging his head against the windscreen. Someone had called an ambulance before he'd regained consciousness, otherwise he would have insisted on being taken the short distance to the *castello* rather than being carted off to hospital. Still, he was here now—he had made sure of that.

There had been no way he was going to spend the night in hospital, attached to machines and being fussed over by well-meaning nurses. Being a good patient meant doing as you were told— something Orlando had always struggled with. And besides, there was nothing wrong with him.

Although being watched like a hawk by Isobel, who was perched on a chair by the side of the bed, was doing nothing for his blood pressure.

Orlando turned his head to see her better as she sat there in the dim glow of the single bed- side lamp. She looked so fragile, her eyes unnatu- rally large, wide green pools of concern that were trained on him, hardly even permitting herself to blink for fear that she might miss some sign that meant he was suffering the onset of catastrophic brain damage.

He hardened his heart. He didn't want her here— not seeing him like this. He hated the way she was making him feel—not just the carnal lust that he had come to accept as a given where Isobel was concerned, but something deeper, something more profound. Something that stirred inside him when he thought about her.

Strong, independent Isobel, who had faced his demands with courage and determination. Beautiful Isobel, who was looking at him now with such tenderness that it made him want to…to what? Throw back the covers and march away, off into the darkness, to put as much space between them as he could? Or to take her in his arms and tenderly make love to her all night long? Regrettably, neither of those things would be happening.

'I want you to go, Isobel, leave me in peace.' His voice sounded harsh—cruel, even. 'You need to get some sleep…you look exhausted.'

'I'm not leaving you, Orlando.' There she went again, displaying that stubborn, wilful streak that drove him so crazy. 'You have to be watched for twenty-four hours.'

'And what exactly are you watching *for*?' Irritation spiked inside him as he gazed at the soft pout of her lips, the drugging depths of her eyes.

'Loss of consciousness, deafness, weakness in arms or legs, vomiting…' She counted off the symptoms on the slender white fingers held up before her. Somehow she even managed to make those words sound sexy. 'Oh, and drowsiness—though I suppose that would be expected at this time of night.'

'You seem to know a lot about it.' He spoke with weary sarcasm, turning his head on the pillow.

Isobel hesitated, her shoulders dropping as she leant back in the chair. 'I should do.' Her voice dropped low. 'I've had concussion myself.'

'You have? 'Orlando narrowed his eyes, grateful to switch the focus to Isobel. 'When was that?'

'Um…a car crash, when I was seventeen.' Her hands twisted in her lap.

'What happened?'

'It doesn't matter.'

'What *happened*, Isobel?'

Isobel hesitated, anguish flooding her face. 'My father died.' Her voice was soft but defiant. 'That's what happened.'

'*Dio,* I'm very sorry to hear that.' Orlando eased himself more upright. 'Do you want to tell me about it?'

'No, I don't.'

'Look, this is going to be a long night.' He paused, judging how best to continue. 'We might as well use it to get to know one another.'

'Even if we don't like what we discover?'

'That's a risk we'll have to take.'

Bold words, because Orlando knew full well he had no intention of baring his soul to this young woman. But he *did* want to know more about the enigma that was Isobel—much more. The virgin temptress who had driven him mad with desire from their very first meeting…the hotshot business woman whose ambition and determination shone through, but whose vulnerability was only beginning to come to the surface… Suddenly he wanted to find out everything he could about the mother of his child.

'You might change your mind when you find out what I did. Because *I* caused the accident—it was all *my* fault.' The words came out in a rush of pain and she raised her chin, daring him to challenge her.

'Your fault?' He repeated the words, watching the suffering that was contorting Isobel's features. But he wasn't going to ignore the challenge—especially as his every instinct was telling him she had to be mistaken.

'Yes. The car crash, my father's death, my mother's subsequent disabilities—it was all my fault.'

'Go on.'

Isobel shot him a rebellious, grief-stricken stare. He could see her tussling with her conscience and her pride, sense just how painful it was for her to talk about this. But he wasn't going to let her off the hook. They had come this far. He had no intention of letting the moment pass.

'I'm waiting.'

'We were travelling on the motorway.' Finally Isobel let herself begin, dropping her shoulders, lowering her eyes to her lap. 'My parents were arguing. They argued a lot. I don't even remember what this one was about.'

Her voice was hollow, cutting through the shadows of the room.

'Anger was making my father drive far too fast, and then my mother started to hit him, beating her fists against him so that the car started to swerve into the path of a bus full of passengers. I shouted at them from the back seat, but they took no notice. I thought I had to do something, so I...'

'What did you do, Isobel?'

'I unbuckled my seat belt and leant forward to grab the steering wheel. I thought I could get the car back into the right lane, but my angle was wrong, and the speed was too great, and we crashed straight into the central reservation. My father was killed instantly.'

Her voice cracked into silence.

Several seconds passed. The terror of the ordeal Isobel had suffered was playing across her shadowed features as clearly as if it were happening now. Orlando felt a strange helplessness, a plunging sensation, like an elevator in free fall. He didn't know how or why, but suddenly he knew he had to do something to try to ease that pain. But first he needed all the facts.

He cleared his throat. 'And what about you?' He kept his tone deliberately neutral. 'Apart from the concussion, did you have any other injuries?'

'A few cuts and bruises.' She attempted a throwaway shrug. 'Remarkably little, considering. My mother was not so lucky. She had to have several operations on her legs. Physically she should have recovered, but mentally she couldn't cope with the trauma. She has been in a wheelchair ever since.'

'And the bus? Were any other vehicles involved?' Still he delved for the truth.

'No.'

'And supposing you hadn't taken the wheel when you did? Supposing you had crashed into the bus? Wouldn't that have been far worse?'

'Well, nobody knows, but—'

'Listen to me, Isobel. In no way am I trying to denigrate your father's death, or underestimate the hideous trauma that you have suffered, but this guilt…you have to let it go.' He was sitting upright now, his back straight, the pains of his bruised body forgotten, as nothing compared to Isobel's suffering. He reached forward to take one of her hands in his. It felt very small and light, almost lifeless. 'Do you hear me?'

Isobel looked down at her hand, then raised her sea-green eyes to meet his.

'But how can I ever forgive myself when even my own mother cannot forgive me?'

'Your *mother*?'

'Yes. She blames me for what happened. For killing her husband, for ruining her life.'

'That's ridiculous. If they hadn't been fighting the accident would never have happened.'

Isobel gave a light shrug. 'It was *my* fault, Orlando. You have no idea how this feels—how could you?'

Oh, but he could. He knew how it felt, all right. Wasn't he eaten up with guilt himself? Hadn't he been carrying the burden of Sophia's death all these years, no matter how much he had tried to ignore it? Come to that, wasn't he the worst person to be offering Isobel advice?

And now Isobel was looking at him with beseeching eyes, wanting him to ease her suffering, to heal her pain. Didn't she realise that he could never be that person? Didn't she realise that getting close to him—emotionally close—would only bring more sorrow and despair?

Dropping her hand, he lay back against the pillow and closed his eyes, determined to blot her out, to protect her from himself.

'Life is tough, Isobel.' He knew his voice sounded harsh, callous. 'Stuff happens...things don't work out the way we planned. We just have to deal with it as best we can.'

A cold silence settled like a blanket of snow, broken by a small sniff. Opening his eyes, Orlando saw that Isobel was still looking at him, tears brimming in her eyes, sliding quietly down her cheeks. And it all but crucified him.

CHAPTER TEN

FUMBLING FOR THE box of tissues, Isobel dabbed her eyes, then blew her nose noisily. For heaven's sake, what did she think she was *doing*, bursting into tears like this? She was supposed to be the strong one here, the one taking charge. But the more she tried to stop the wretched tears, the faster they wanted to come, until they ended up blocking her throat, producing a guttural gurgling sound that had Orlando staring at her in alarm.

Why had she told Orlando about the accident and opened the floodgate on her tears? Whatever had made her share her deepest, darkest secret with him? The guilt that had shaped her, tortured her all her adult life. The guilt that she had never spoken about to anyone—ever. Not even her mother. *Especially not her mother.*

But, sitting beside Orlando in the dark confessional of this castle bedroom, she had felt the strangest of sensations come over her: an overwhelming need to confess her most harrowing of secrets to him. And now, in answer to her own question, she knew why. It was because she *trusted* Orlando. This realisation had sprung from nowhere, but once lodged in her brain she knew it to be true with an instinctive, unwavering certainty.

She trusted Orlando more than anyone she had ever known, more than anyone else on this planet. *Orlando.* Strong, authoritative, demanding. Intelligent, inscrutable and infuriating. All of those things. But honourable too, upright and decent and determined to do the best for his child. Isobel knew she would trust him with her life—more than that, she would trust him with her darkest of secrets.

And her instinct had been right. Orlando hadn't met her confession with the sign of the cross and banished her from the room. He hadn't judged her, or offered misplaced sympathies or platitudes. In true Orlando style he had merely ascertained the facts, reviewed them, and then pronounced his judgement. And for one light-headed moment Isobel had felt the guilt starting to lift, the weight rising from her shoulders.

Only to have it replaced with the burden of his next crushing statement.

Stuff happens... We just have to deal with it as best we can.

The words still rang in Isobel's ears. She had no doubt as to what he'd been talking about. She and the baby were the *stuff* and that was what Orlando was doing—dealing with it. He had used this beautiful *castello* as a means to an end—the lure that he'd needed to stop her prevaricating and commit to making a family home together. Except it would never be that...not in the true sense of the

word. In reality it was little more than a prison—
for both of them.

And this was the brutal fact that had made the
tears flow.

'Isobel?' Propping himself up on his elbow, Orlando tried to look at her.

Blowing her nose again, Isobel turned away.

'Isobel, what's the matter?' He stretched out to
reach her, his hand grasping her upper arm. 'What
is it?'

'Nothing.'

'Look at you. You are shaking.'

It was true—she was. The trauma of Orlando's
accident followed by the emotional outpouring of
her confession and then the cruelty of Orlando's
callous remark meant her overloaded body couldn't
take any more and had started to shiver, the trem-
ors spreading up her arms to the slender shoulders
that now shook alarmingly.

'Isobel. Speak to me.'

Pulling back the covers, Orlando swung his legs
over the bed. Isobel caught the flash of lean muscled flesh, the white of his boxer shorts, before she
lowered her eyes to her lap.

'Do you need a doctor?'

'No, no. I'm not ill.' Wrapping her arms around
herself, she tilted her chin, knowing she had to
meet his worried gaze. He was leaning in close
now, seated on the edge of bed with his hands on

his bare thighs, poised, as if ready to take whatever action he deemed necessary.

'It's just been a very long day, that's all.' She drew in a shuddering breath.

It certainly had. Long and traumatic and at times mind-numbingly terrifying.

When Maria had first told her about the accident Isobel had been afraid that the devastating shock would render her unable to function at all. But somehow she had managed to rouse herself, pure adrenaline keeping her heart pumping and giving her the strength to get to the hospital.

Sitting in the car next to an anxious-looking Pietro, she had felt as if she was living a nightmare. Because this accident was her fault too. It had to be. This was what happened when she loved someone…they died. First her father and now Orlando… History was cruelly repeating itself.

But Orlando hadn't died. He was here, flesh and blood, all magnificent six-foot-plus of him, a little bruised and bloodied, but still his normal forceful, macho self. Very much alive.

And the relief had been too enormous for words. Like an aftershock it had flooded through her, weakening her bones still further, draining what little resistance she had.

'*Certamente*. And it has been made considerably longer by my having this stupid accident.'

With his head on one side he peered at her. 'I'm sorry, Isobel.'

'It was hardly your fault. Yours or the deer's.' *Oh, no.* At the thought of that poor deer she could feel the tears building up again.

Pushing himself to stand, Orlando tugged the cover off the bed, then leant forward to drape it over Isobel's shoulders. 'Here—this will stop you shivering.'

Holding the cover under her chin with one hand, he bent down until his face was just inches from her own, the large swelling on his head clearly visible. Isobel closed her eyes against the soft assault of his breath, the masculine heat emanating from his body.

'You need to go to bed, Isobel, get some rest.'

'I'm not leaving you alone, Orlando.' She fought to open her eyes again. 'The doctor said…'

'I don't give a damn what the doctor said. You look utterly exhausted and you are obviously seriously overwrought. I am not going to be responsible for the breakdown of your health—nor for putting our baby at risk, come to that.'

'And *I* am not going to be responsible for *you* having brain damage.'

Pulling the bedcover closer around her, Isobel retaliated with as much force as she could muster. Orlando scowled, his eyes darting across her obstinate face, his mouth opening and then closing again.

'Very well.'

He pulled himself upright and Isobel found herself staring at the waistband of his boxer shorts, the jut of his hips, the line of dark hair descending from his navel. She swallowed.

'In that case we will have to reach a compromise. You will have to get into bed with me.'

Isobel stared as he walked stiffly around the bed, pulling back the sheet and rearranging the pillows.

'I can't.' Isobel felt the breath catch in her throat. 'I mean…you have just been in an accident…'

'I'm suggesting we lie quietly side by side, Isobel, nothing else.'

'No, of course not.' Isobel felt herself blush, glad that the dim light in the room hid her embarrassment. 'But I still think it would be better if I stayed here in the…'

'Get in.' It was an order now, barked from the other side of the bed, where he stood all lean, shadowed muscle and impatient glowering. 'You really don't want to make me force you, do you? Not in my present injured condition?'

Isobel lowered her eyes, away from the oh-so-seductive image before her. She knew getting into bed with Orlando was the last thing she should do, but she felt so tired…so overwhelmingly, debilitatingly tired…as if her bones had turned to lead, and suddenly it seemed like the most tempting thing in the world.

Before giving herself any more time to think she stood up, unfastened her sandals and moved to the side of the bed. Orlando watched her, waiting with exaggerated patience, one arm extended to indicate the space he had made for her.

'I would suggest removing some clothes—unless you want to make me feel seriously under-dressed.'

Isobel looked down at herself. She was still wearing the jeans and T-shirt she had put on that morning in London. Was it really possible that what seemed like a lifetime ago had actually been the same day? Taking in a breath, she quickly undid her jeans and tugged them off, leaving them on the floor beside her.

She found herself wishing she wasn't wearing such skimpy lace knickers at the same time as she asked herself what it mattered. After all, Orlando had made it quite clear that this was nothing more than a practical arrangement. But with his eyes mercilessly raking over her she decided that was as far as her strip was going and, jumping into bed, pulled the sheet up to her chin and lay very, very still.

'That's better.' She felt him climb in beside her, moving his body around to try to get comfortable. 'At least this way you will get some rest, even if you refuse to sleep. And should anything untoward happen to me during the night you will be the first to know.'

'That isn't funny, Orlando.' Anger spiked through her anxiety and she turned to slant him a furious look. Propped up against the pillows, he had linked his hands behind his head, defining the pectoral muscles of his bare chest and cording the tendons of his forearms. He looked nothing like the invalid he was supposed to be. 'You've been in a serious accident. You could have been *killed*.'

'I know. *Mi dispiace...* I'm sorry.'

Careful not to meet his eyes, for fear of what she might see there, Isobel turned back, shifting across the bed to make sure there was a decent space between them. Then she gazed up at the ceiling.

'Are you going to turn off the light?' he asked.

'Um...yes.' Reaching across, Isobel did as she was asked.

Silence reigned.

Isobel could hear Orlando's breathing—soft, rhythmic, seductive. Squirming as little as possible, she adjusted the T-shirt that had twisted under her. Squeezing her eyes closed, she flatly refused to let her body succumb to his nearness. Even if every nerve ending was screaming at her that he was lying virtually naked only inches from her, she didn't have to listen. She could block out the throb of awareness, the pulsing, masculine virility that surrounded him, charging the small gap between them like a force field. She could block out the physical yearning to feel his arms around her if she really tried.

She would just keep calm and stay alert for any changes in his condition. Perhaps she would match the rhythm of his breathing with her own. In…out. She felt the tension in her body start to lessen, her eyelids grow heavy. In…out…

Orlando stared at the sleeping beauty next to him. Several hours had passed and now dawn was starting to break. A new day. He wanted to move, desperately needed to shift his position to ease the stiffness in his spine, the aching of his limbs. But moving would disturb Isobel, and right now he couldn't bear to do that.

Having finally persuaded her to get into bed with him, much to his surprise he had seen her fall asleep almost immediately. And in the oblivion of sleep she had turned towards him, curling her body against his, flinging out one arm so that it rested across his chest, her hand lightly settled on his shoulder.

She looked so peaceful, so innocent, but the rush of tenderness he felt towards her twisted his heart. Because he knew he could never be the man he wanted to be for her. He was too damaged, too scarred.

When she had finally opened up about the car accident, the way her father had died, he had felt her pain like a punch in the gut, and the anguish swirling in her beautiful green eyes had threatened to undo him completely. More than anything he had wanted to help her, to reach out and take away her misery and grief, to protect her from the pain, from all the agonies that life could throw at her. But what right did he have to do that? Him of all people? He who was riddled with demons of his own—demons he had no intention of exposing to Isobel or anyone else.

He didn't have Isobel's courage to come clean, but he refused to be a fraud. So what had he done? Cruelly ended the conversation. Shut her down. Made her cry. Because that was the man he was, the only man he could ever be.

Looking down at Isobel now, he lightly brushed a strand of silky hair away from her face. Her eyelids flickered, the dark lashes twitching, then settling against her cheek. He knew only too well that he had turned her life upside down—first by getting her pregnant and then by insisting that she came to live with him. Like a rag doll in the mouth of a Rottweiler she had been shaken until she had dropped at his feet.

Except Isobel was no rag doll—far from it. Yes,

he had managed to bend her to his will, but it was Isobel's courage that had made her agree to his terms, not weakness. She was the feistiest, most independent young woman he had ever met. And he loved that about her. He loved a lot of things about her.

Which made his next decision even harder. He was going to insist they got married right away.

Despite his attempt to make light of his accident—both to himself and to Isobel—the fact was it had shaken him up. Not in the physical sense— he'd been lucky, nothing more than a bump and a few bruises, and he knew perfectly well that all Isobel's concerns were unfounded. But the accident had made him face up to his own mortality.

Supposing he hadn't been so lucky? Supposing it had been him lying glassy-eyed in a ditch instead of the stag?

He and Isobel had to get married *now*—as soon as possible. He wasn't prepared to wait any longer. If he had died in that crash, where would that have left his child? Not only fatherless, but with no legal rights whatsoever—not to his business empire, the Trevente estate or the title of Marchese di Trevente. Nothing. And, worse still, an earlier bit of research had revealed that his child wouldn't even have been able to take the Cassano name. Legally, with an unmarried couple, the father had to be there in person to register the birth in order for his name to go on the birth certificate. Either that or it would have to be authorised by the courts, as had been the pitiful situation with his own father. But both of those were clearly impossible if you were dead.

Orlando would have been erased from his child's life as if he had never existed. And suddenly he knew he sure as hell wasn't going to let that happen.

Isobel stirred against him, her lips parting in sleep as if she was going to say something, then settling again into an adorable pout.

There was another reason Orlando wanted to move the wedding forward. One that he had to force himself to acknowledge. Supposing Isobel changed her mind? She had agreed to marry him at some unspecified date in the future, but what was to say that she wouldn't have a change of heart? Or that she'd never really planned to go through with it in the first place, just agreeing to get him off her back? Or, worse still…and this thought had clawed its talons into Orlando's skin, made his hands ball into fists…supposing she met someone else?

It was possible…it could happen. Isobel was an extremely attractive young woman and Orlando had seen the way men looked at her. And now they were in Italy, where every man was convinced he was a red-hot lover and would leap at the opportunity to prove it.

Turning slightly, he felt Isobel's hand tighten on his shoulder. His own body tightened in response. It would be so easy to plant a kiss on those pink lips, to wait for her reaction, for her to mould herself against him, invite him to make love to her in the way his body had already pre-empted, evident in the growing erection that he was fighting to ignore.

'You are so beautiful, Isobel. Have I ever told you that?'

Lowering his head, Orlando whispered the words so quietly he wasn't sure if they were even audible. He wanted to make love to her so badly it hurt. But sex solved nothing—no matter how good it felt at the time.

So instead he lifted her arm and laid it gently by her side. Then, inching back the covers, he ordered himself to creep away from her delectably warm and sleeping body. It was time to take a very long, very cold shower.

You are so beautiful, Isobel.

The words floated around inside her head, repeating themselves over and over until Isobel found herself smiling, reaching out for Orlando to reassure herself that he was there.

Except he wasn't.

Waking from her lovely dream with a jolt, Isobel found the bed beside her empty. Panic immediately gripped her. What time was it? She squinted at the watch she still had on her wrist. Nine fifteen! How on earth had she slept that long? How had she fallen asleep at all? She was supposed to have been watching over Orlando. What if something terrible had happened to him?

Pulling on a robe over the crumpled T-shirt, Isobel dashed out into the corridor, looking both ways before starting to run down the stairs, her mind already conjuring up hideously dramatic images of him lying comatose on the floor somewhere, a resuscitation team desperately trying to bring him back to life.

It was a scenario only made a thousand times worse when through the window she caught sight of a recovery truck towing the crumpled wreck of Orlando's sports car up the long driveway. She couldn't bear to look at it.

But the window at the next turn of the stairs revealed something else. A flash of sunshine on water and there, cutting long, slow strokes from one end of the swimming pool to the other, was Orlando.

Returning to the bedroom, Isobel sat on the edge of the bed, waiting for her heart rate to steady, for the awful image of that mangled car to disappear. She would take a quick shower, get dressed, and then go and give him a piece of her mind.

He was out of the water and towelling himself dry when Isobel finally arrived at the poolside.

'*What* do you think you are doing?' Placing her hands on her hips, she squinted up at him. 'You are supposed to be in bed.'

She watched as he wrapped the towel low around his hips, staring at the beads of water that were clinging to the taut planes of his chest, at the bruises shadowing his olive skin.

'I decided to christen the pool.' Crossing his arms, Orlando fixed her with an inscrutable stare.

'Well, you shouldn't have done. Not without telling me.'

'You were sound asleep, as I recall.'

Isobel scowled back at him.

'I thought a swim might help with the stiffness.' Unfolding his arms Orlando stretched his back, then rolled his shoulders one after the other, several times. 'I think it's worked.'

'Well, that's good, I suppose.' Isobel swallowed. 'I can see there is quite a bit of bruising on your left-hand side.' She hesitated, then took a step closer to him. 'How does your head feel today?'

Before she could stop herself her hand had risen to brush aside a lock of damp hair, her fingers lightly tracing the injury with a feather-light trembling softness.

For a moment they stared at each other, the silence broken only by the friendly chirrup of a bird in a nearby tree.

'It's fine.' Finally Orlando spoke. 'Just a bump.'

'It does look better, I must say.' Isobel let her hand drop awkwardly by her side. 'The swelling has gone down. But I think you ought to see a doctor today.'

'Already arranged.' Sweeping the stray locks back from his forehead, Orlando raked a hand through his wet hair. 'He'll be here in half an hour or so. I thought it would put your mind at rest, if nothing else.'

'That's good.' Isobel looked down at Orlando's bare feet, at his footprints that were rapidly drying in the morning sun. 'I'm glad to see you being responsible at last.'

'Oh, I can be *responsible*, Isobel.'

Moving a couple of paces away, he picked up a pair of jeans that were lying by the pool and after unceremoniously dropping the towel started to tug them on. Isobel tore her gaze away.

'In fact my sense of responsibility has led me to an important conclusion.'

'Really?' She wasn't going to look back until she was sure he was decent. 'What conclusion?'

Flies buttoned, he was beside her again, looping his arm around her bare shoulders. Isobel felt the cold weight of it making her skin tingle as he turned her to walk back towards the *castello*.

'The accident yesterday…' Orlando spoke softly. 'I realise now that you were right. I shouldn't have dismissed it so lightly. Life can be cut short very quickly.' He slanted her a glance. 'Something *you* know only too well.'

Isobel nodded, not trusting herself to speak.

'For that reason I think we should get married.'

'Well, I know that.' Isobel continued purposefully putting one foot in front of the other, the newly mown grass springy beneath her feet. 'We've agreed that after the baby is born—'

'Not after the baby is born, Isobel. I mean straight away.'

They stopped. Orlando's eyes raked across her face as he waited for her reply, commanding her to agree.

'Straight away?' Isobel blinked against the sheer force of his power. 'Why?'

'Because I want our child to be legally protected *now*, not leave it to chance any longer. After what happened yesterday I am not prepared to take that risk any more.' His voice was quietly controlled, but it held that familiar hint of steel. 'We marry now, Isobel. It's the only solution.'

Isobel sucked in a breath, recognising that once again she was being manipulated by Orlando Cassano. Now it seemed he was determined to override her last stand.

And that was all it was. A pointless exercise

in proving that she had some control. Although maybe there was *one* other reason—something it was high time she faced up to and then buried for ever.

By delaying the wedding she had been hoping that Orlando might change his mind. Not about marrying her, but about his reasons for doing so. She had been pathetically waiting for a sign that Orlando might want to marry her for who she was, not just because she was the mother of his child. Well, she was done with that now. She had to accept it was never going to happen. She had to accept the stark reality of the situation and try and focus on the positives.

A few short hours ago she had been terrified that Orlando was dead, and yet here he was, strong and proud and as controlling as ever. She thanked God for that. And she accepted that he wanted what was best for their child. Their child, at least, obviously meant a great deal to him. Even if *she* meant nothing. If Orlando wanted to marry now, what difference did it make? To insist on waiting for a few months would be nothing more than churlish.

Turning away, Isobel started heading back towards the *castello* again, leaving Orlando in her wake.

'If that's what you want, Orlando, I will agree.' She tossed the words over her shoulder. 'We can have the wedding as soon as you like.'

CHAPTER ELEVEN

FROM ISOBEL'S BEDROOM window there was a perfect view of the wedding venue. Rows of white chairs were neatly laid out on the grass in front of the twinkling lake, where an archway covered with pink and white roses had been positioned. The place where she and Orlando would very shortly be standing to make their vows. Isobel stared at the scene with disbelieving eyes, still not able to fully comprehend that she was marrying Orlando at all—let alone that it would be happening in an hour's time.

Tearing her eyes away, she retreated into the room.

It had been agreed that she should move into her own suite of rooms two weeks ago, leaving Orlando in the master bedroom, ostensibly to recover from his accident.

Isobel still remembered Orlando's expression when he had suggested it—guarded, wary, as if he were telling a young child it was being sent to boarding school *for its own good*. But he needn't have worried. Isobel had been only too happy to give them both some space, because sharing a bed every night with Orlando would have been torture. Whether they had made love or not made love—both would have been equally agonising. Both would have had the power to break her heart.

Just living in the *castello* with him had been bad enough: the forced politeness, the quickly eaten meals, with one or other of them hurrying to excuse themselves to 'get on with some work'. Since the night of the accident it had felt as if Orlando had deliberately constructed a wall between them, as if he was determined to keep her out.

Walking over to the bed, she stared at the wedding dress that was carefully laid across it. Picking it up by the hanger, she held it before her. It was beautiful—too beautiful. Chosen on a day trip to Milan with Maria and her teenage daughter, Elena. Isobel had opted for a simple style in cream silk. The strapless bodice was decorated with tiny seed pearls and the sweeping skirt fell in fluid folds to the floor. Maria and Elena had clasped their hands to their chests in unison when she had stepped from the dressing room, immediately declaring it *'molto bella'.*

There was a tap on the door now, and a beaming Elena entered, a small bunch of roses in her hand.

'The guests will be arriving soon, Isobel. Mamma—she says it is time for me to help you dress.'

'*Grazie*, Elena— thank you.'

'I have some flowers left over from the decorations. I am thinking maybe we could put them in your hair?'

Isobel glanced at Elena. Already dressed in her wedding outfit, she looked so pretty, so happy, so excited about today. At seventeen years old, she was the same age Isobel had been when the car crash had all but decimated her life. Isobel firmly hoped that no such tragedy would ever befall this lovely young woman. She hoped that one day Elena would find her Prince Charming and have a real fairy-tale wedding. Not the sham that she herself was about to go through.

Handing the dress over to Elena, Isobel took off her robe, glancing down at the wedding lingerie that Maria and Elena had made her buy: a strapless bra and flimsy silk panties, a suspender belt with white silk stockings. She felt like a total fraud.

But Elena was waiting, holding up the dress for her to step into, going behind her to fasten the row of tiny pearl buttons. Finally she reached for Isobel's shoes, the cream satin creations that Isobel had had made in the Spicer workshop, giving no hint as to who they were for. Facing her again Elena fussed with the material of the skirt before standing back to admire her handiwork.

'Finito.' She gave Isobel an emotional smile. 'Il Marchese—he is a very lucky man.'

Isobel attempted to smile back, unconsciously smoothing the silky material over her very small baby bump. Reaching forward, Elena took hold of her hands and moved them to her sides. She let them drop, shaking her head.

'You cannot see it, Isobel. Your beautiful secret is safe for today.'

Beautiful secret. Was that what it was?

Nerves, mixed with anxiety and something approaching a sickening dread, gripped Isobel. But Elena was waiting for her, standing by the dressing table now, with a hairbrush in her hand, ready to do her hair. A quick glance through the window showed her that the guests were starting to arrive, the rows of seats rapidly filling up.

Their guest list hadn't been long. Isobel herself had invited no one, apart from her mother, who had declared herself far too unwell to travel. She had friends in London but she didn't want them here—didn't want to involve them in this sham of a marriage. Telling them the truth would have involved too many questions, and lying would simply have been deceitful. Far better to say nothing at all.

And presumably Orlando had felt the same. He had few friends in Italy, and no inclination to fly in friends and business colleagues from around the world, so his guest list mostly comprised tenants and workers on the estate, along with the Cassano family solicitor and a few local dignitaries.

In front of the mirror now, Isobel stared at her

reflection. Pale, but poised, she appeared calm. The creeping doubt did not really show on her face, except perhaps in her eyes, which looked back at her with dull sufferance. This was her wedding day. It was supposed to be the happiest day of her life. Instead she felt as if she was about to go to the gallows.

What on earth was she doing?

A wave of nausea swept over her, draining what little colour she had from her face as the full reality of what she was about to do crushed her chest with its leaden, oppressive weight. *She was about to marry a man whom she loved with all her heart, but who would never love her back.* The stark reality stole the breath from her lungs, slowed her heart rate to a leaden beat.

These past couple of weeks she had allowed herself to be swept along with the wedding preparations, convincing herself with a mixture of naivety and hope that it would be all right, that somehow it would all work out. Now, with the bruising clarity of a knockout blow, she knew that wasn't the case. She couldn't do this. She couldn't subject herself to the misery of a loveless marriage—not feeling the way she did about Orlando. Being around him would be too painful, too agonisingly raw, like exposing her heart to a thousand cuts. Marrying Orlando would be sentencing herself to a lifetime of torment.

Sudden dizziness made her clutch for the edge of the dressing table and she saw Elena's eyes widen with alarm.

'Could you get me a glass of water, please, Elena?'

'Sì, certo.'

Elena hurried off to the bathroom, and Isobel found herself staring blankly into the space she had left. She needed to think quickly—work out what she was going to do. But her brain seemed to be stuffed with cotton wool, refusing to process simple commands.

'Here.' Pressing a glass into her hand, Elena looked down at her with concerned eyes. 'You have the nerves, I expect. Drink this and you will feel better.'

Raising the glass to her lips, Isobel watched the water ripple beneath her shaky grasp. *Come on, Isobel, get a grip—do something now, before it's too late.*

'Better now?'

She saw her reflection nod, and a relieved Elena went back to fiddling with her hair.

Find Orlando. Isobel desperately tried to order her thoughts. That was what she had to do first. She must find Orlando and explain to him that she couldn't marry him. He would be livid, furious beyond words, but that couldn't be helped. For the sake of her future sanity she had to do this.

The wedding was off.

'Orlando... Il Marchese,' she began slowly. 'Do you know where he is, Elena?'

Elena shook her head, then took a rose out of her mouth to allow herself to speak. 'No, not exactly at the moment.'

Isobel noticed that she didn't quite meet her eyes in the mirror. Another, different fear gripped her.

'When was he last seen?'

'Um... Papà—he saw him this morning.' Standing back, she tweaked the position of the cream rose she had tucked into the swept up tresses of Isobel's hair. 'There—what do you think?'

'Saw him where, exactly?' Spinning round in her seat, Isobel faced Elena full-on.

'Papà...he say Il Marchese ask him to bring round the saloon car from the garage.'

'To take him where? Where was he going, Elena?'

'He say he was going to the airport.'

The airport? Gripping the edge of the stool, Isobel pulled herself to her feet.

'He probably had to meet someone. A guest, maybe?'

Or he had boarded a flight to the US and was now thousands of feet above them in the sky.

With her heart thumping beneath the constricting bodice, Isobel forced herself to try and calm down. She was being ridiculous. Why would Orlando run away? He was the one who wanted this, who had insisted that it happened. And yet still the panic refused to subside.

'I'm sure you are right, Elena.' Her voice sounded odd, as if it was coming from far away. 'Thank you so much for your help, but if you don't mind I think I would like to be left alone now.'

Reaching the door, Elena looked back over her shoulder with a reassuring smile. 'I am sure there is nothing to worry about, Isobel. Il Marchese—he will be here in time for the ceremony.'

Drumming his fingers on the steering wheel, Orlando glanced at his watch. Two-forty-five. In precisely fifteen minutes he was supposed to be getting married—slipping a wedding ring onto Isobel's finger and finally making her his. Securing their future together. But right now he felt as if everything was conspiring against him. The final straw being this wretched traffic jam they had been stuck in for the past twenty minutes.

His morning from hell had started when Astrid, his personal assistant in London, had informed him that Mrs Nancy Spicer *wouldn't* be flying to Trevente for the wedding after all. It seemed that the private jet he had sent for her, and indeed the car he had dispatched to pick her up from the nursing home, were no longer needed. Mrs Spicer had changed her mind. She was staying put.

Orlando should have left it at that, but he was far too stubborn to accept defeat. And this was more than just stubbornness. When Isobel had lightly informed him that her mother wouldn't be attending the wedding he had seen the hurt in her eyes, and that had been enough for Orlando. He was going to do this one thing for Isobel. He was going to make this happen.

So, refusing to accept the initial setback, he had caught a flight to London, arrived at Nancy Spicer's nursing home and persuaded her to come back with him on his private jet—all without too much trouble. It seemed the personal touch had been all that was needed. *His* personal touch, at any rate.

Time had been getting tight, but at that point Orlando had been confident they were going to make it. Then problems with air traffic control had delayed their flight and they had ended up spending a frustrating hour sitting on the runway.

Never one to miss an opportunity, Orlando had used the time to raise the subject of the fatal car crash with his future mother-in-law—the tragedy that had so decimated the Spicer family. It had been playing on his mind ever since Isobel had told him about it; her haunted expression, the depth of the pain, had been a knife in his soul.

Initially shocked, then hostile, then defensive, Mrs Spicer had refused to discuss the subject with him. But Orlando had said his piece, firmly pointing out that blaming Isobel for what had happened was doing neither of them any good. And he was confident that his message had hit home, no matter how much this proud woman refused to acknowledge it.

When they had finally landed in Le Marche, Orlando had settled Mrs Spicer into the back of his car, intending on a fast dash back to the *castello*. But that idea had been scotched when she had imperiously informed him that she refused to travel in a speeding car. Either he slowed down or she got out.

Like mother, like daughter. Suddenly Isobel's extreme reaction to his driving had made perfect sense.

Now this traffic jam was the final straw. Orlando felt like getting out of the car himself, running the last ten miles to the *castello* with his future mother-in-law on his back if he had to. Impatience and something more worrying furrowed his brow. There was a nagging feeling in his gut that something wasn't right—not just his lateness, but something more serious.

Reaching for his phone, he tried dialling the *castello* landline again, but there was still no answer. They must all be outside, waiting for the ceremony to start. Suddenly he desperately wanted to speak to Isobel, to reassure her that he was on his way. Just to hear her voice.

Tossing the phone onto the seat beside him he cursed yet again at the lack of mobile signal at the *castello*. Why hadn't he got that sorted?

Hearing the blaring of horns behind him, Orlando glanced in the rearview mirror and caught a glimpse of Nancy Spicer, applying another coat of red lipstick. Snapping her compact shut she glared at him.

'Well, hurry up, then.' She waved her arm impatiently. 'Can't you see the traffic is moving again?'

Left alone in her bedroom, Isobel gathered her skirts around her and drew in a painful breath. A glance at the clock revealed that it was almost three o'clock. The ceremony was due to start at any moment. Pushing open her window she leaned out, staring at the rows of wedding guests, at the officiant who was now standing under the rose-covered bower, checking his watch. She could hear the melodious sound of Vivaldi being played by the string quartet, the chatter of the guests' voices, laughter, a baby crying. But there was no sign of the groom.

Closing the window, Isobel turned her back on the scene. She felt numb, completely detached from the proceedings going on outside—as if none of it was remotely real.

She moved back to the bed and sat down, looking blankly around her. Hot tears were starting to scald the back of her eyes but she would not let them fall. What difference did it make if Orlando had decided he couldn't go through with the marriage? Hadn't she decided the same thing? Logically, she should be pleased. This was probably the first thing they had ever agreed on.

But logic refused to convince her poor broken heart. She could feel it twisting inside her now, beating to a painful, jerky rhythm that made her wonder if each pulse was going to be its last. She desperately wanted to be strong, but sitting there, staring down at the silky folds of her beautiful wedding gown, she barely had the strength to breathe.

She felt hollow, frozen with misery, and terribly, terribly alone. And the worst of it was that the only person who could comfort her was the man who was causing this pain. Orlando. She wanted him beside her so badly it was like a physical ache. She wanted him to take her in his arms and tell her that everything would be all right. She wanted him to say that he loved her the way she loved him— deeply, profoundly, and with a passion that would never, ever die.

But that was never going to happen. Drawing in a breath that snagged in her throat like silk in the teeth of a saw, Isobel tried to think what to do.

She couldn't just stay here, waiting for a groom who wasn't going to show in order to tell him she couldn't marry him. It didn't get much more ridiculous than that. Or more heartbreakingly tragic. A strange sort of light-headedness came over her, as if her poor frazzled brain couldn't work out what was important any more so had given up and poured itself a large drink.

Rising to her feet, Isobel felt herself wobble. She needed some fresh air—to get away from this room where the walls were starting to close in on her. She needed some time to decide what to do.

There was no one around when Isobel emerged and scanned the long corridor. She could hear a phone ringing far below, somewhere on the ground floor, but nobody was rushing to answer it. Even so, she decided not to go down there and run the risk of bumping into Maria, or Elena, or some other well-meaning person. She could already see the pity in their eyes, hear their sympathetic platitudes.

Picking up her skirts, she suddenly knew where she would go—she would climb up to the tower. No one ever went up there except her, and with luck there would be a cooling breeze. The tower was her favourite place—the one part of the *castello* so far left unrestored by the builders, complicated Italian bureaucracy meaning they had to wait for permission before they could so much as replace a single stone of the medieval battlements.

After ducking under the arched doorway, she straightened up again, sucking in the glorious fresh air. She had been right about the breeze. It whipped across her cheeks, tugging at the pins that held her hair, billowing the skirt around her legs. Above her head the Trevente flag cracked like a whip at the top of its flagpole.

Moving further into the space, Isobel stood and gazed around her. There was a whole world going on down there. People, families, problems and triumphs, happiness and sadness. She needed to put things into perspective. Stop dwelling on her own problems and focus on doing the best she could with the crazy situation she now found herself in. Focus on making a good life for herself and her child.

People didn't die of a broken heart, despite what it might feel like now. Somehow she would get through this.

Finally Orlando pulled the car up in front of the *castello*. Taking the wheelchair out of the boot and around to the side of the car, he was surprised to see Mrs Spicer already easing herself out, straightening her spine with a pained but determined expression.

'I think I will walk. If I could just take your arm?'

'*Sì, certo*. But the ceremony is being held beside the lake, around the other side of the *castello*. It might be quicker to use the wheelchair.'

'We are so late already, what difference will a few minutes make? Besides, after your little lecture I thought you would be all in favour of me making the effort.' She shot him a haughty stare. 'If I am to give my daughter away, I intend to do it standing on my own two legs. Pass me my stick.'

Orlando gritted his teeth as they made their painfully slow way around the side of the *castello*, across the lawns towards the lake. He could feel his heart thumping heavily in his chest, nerves twisting inside him. Was it only his lateness that was making him so agitated? He just wanted to deliver this cantankerous woman to her front row seat, dash upstairs to change into his suit and then be in position so that the ceremony could finally start.

But mostly he just wanted to see Isobel. To banish this clawing, gnawing feeling that something was wrong.

Cheers greeted them when they finally arrived at the lakeside, where the party seemed to have started without them. In true Italian style the guests were chattering and laughing noisily over the sound of the string quartet, obviously little bothered that the ceremony should have started well over an hour ago. The officiant came towards them, smiling as he shook Orlando's hand. Only Maria looked worried, jumping up from her seat, her round face flushed beneath a wide-brimmed hat decorated with feathers.

'Oh, Il Marchese, I am so pleased that you are here at last.'

'Maria, if you could look after Signora Spicer for me?' Orlando lowered Isobel's mother on to a chair, then stood and looked around him. 'Where is Isobel?'

'She *was* in her room…' Maria spoke with deliberate care.

Of course she was. What had he expected? That she would be standing out here in full view of everyone, waiting for him to turn up?

'But when Elena went up there a few minutes ago…' Maria hesitated, shooting a sideways glance at Mrs Spicer '…she had gone.'

Gone? Switching to Italian, Orlando started to fire rapid questions at Maria, and then Elena, who had come over to join them. Scarcely waiting for their replies, he was already turning, walking quickly, and then running towards the *castello*, with only one thought in his head. He had to find Isobel. *Now.*

Bursting through the front doors, he stopped in the hallway. Fear was starting to spread through his body, clawing at his chest and gripping his throat with merciless talons. He could feel the thunderous beat of his heart, hear his ragged breath cutting through the quiet stillness of the air—air that felt horribly empty.

Dragging in a breath, he held it, listening intently for a sound—any sound that might tell him she was there, might take away the dread that was racing through his veins. But all he could hear was the distant clank of metal coming from the kitchens, mocking him with the reminder of a wedding breakfast that increasing desperation was telling him might never take place.

'Isobel!' Tipping back his head, he called her name up the sweeping staircase. It was met with nothing but cold silence. 'Isobel, answer me, damn you!'

Following his own voice, Orlando tore up the stairs two, three at a time, racing from room to room, flinging open doors, still calling her name, his feet thundering into every empty echoing chamber.

Finally he returned to her suite of rooms and stood in the middle of the bedroom, forcing his breath to steady, commanding the logical side of his brain to kick in. His eyes darted around, searching for clues.

He had never been in this room before today, having convinced himself that Isobel needed her space—that they both had to adjust to the challenges of living in the *castello* without adding the temptation of sex. That exquisite pleasure would come later, when they were married, when things had settled down and they had somehow managed to pick their way through the complicated mix of emotions that at the moment made them spark off each other like flint against steel.

Not that that wasn't exciting in itself. These past two weeks the thought of Isobel alone in her bed, with only a few dark stretches of corridor separating them, had tormented him, kept him awake at night and then burnt into his dreams, awakening him with a throbbing erection desperate to be satisfied.

Never, *ever* had he wanted a woman as badly as he wanted Isobel. Several times he had found himself weakening, setting off to find her, to take her in his arms, to claim her lips and make love to her with the searing, scalding intensity that was threatening his sanity.

But every time he had stopped, forced himself to find some self-control. Because no matter how urgent his desire, how fiercely the longing galloped through his body, he knew he had to think about Isobel—respect her, protect her. He could never offer her more than sex, and common decency refused to let him use her just to satisfy his carnal lust. He cared about her too much for that.

Far too much.

Suddenly the realisation of just what Isobel meant to him slammed into his chest and he sank down onto the bed with his head in his hands. All this time he had been convincing himself that everything he had done was purely for the sake of his unborn child. To provide the stable upbringing that he had never had, to ensure that his son or daughter would want for nothing. Controlling, cajoling, bullying—he had done everything in his power to get Isobel to agree to his terms for the sake of their child.

Or had he? The big, fat lie now stared him in the face, refusing to go away. He *hadn't* done this solely because of the baby. He'd done it because he wanted Isobel in his life—baby or no baby. Because he couldn't imagine his life without her. Because life without her would be empty, dull and depressingly meaningless. Isobel had crept under his skin, infiltrated his mind, body and soul. And one thing was for sure: he wasn't going to lose her now—no way!

Jumping up from the bed, he marched from the room, determination setting his jaw, making him grind his teeth. He was going to find Isobel and he was going to demand that this wedding went ahead. He would *make* it happen.

Pacing the circuit of the battlements, Isobel finally came to a standstill and took in a shuddering breath. The searing pain in her chest hadn't lessened, nor the feeling that life had mysteriously moved on and left her behind. But neither had her conviction that her decision was right—marrying Orlando would have been the biggest mistake of her life. And obviously he felt the same.

With no sign of him it was pathetically, pitifully clear that he had no more intention of going through with the wedding than she did—which only managed to tighten the screws into her heart still further.

Somehow she was going to have to gather the strength to fight her way through this misery and find a way forward. Although right now she had no idea how. Right now she felt as if she had fallen into the deepest darkest well, where she could barely see the hand in front of her face, let alone a pathway ahead.

Pushing the wind-tossed strands of hair away from her face, she gazed up to check that the clear blue sky was still there. Yes, the world was still turning. She was still breathing. And the heart of her precious baby was still pump-pumping away. For that reason alone she would carry on.

When Orlando returned—assuming he ever did—she would insist that they sat down and discussed their future together calmly, like sensible adults. No arguing, no posturing, no pride. *Especially no pride.* Although right now Isobel felt as if she had very little of that left. Somehow they would come up with a solution that they could both live with—a compromise. Something that didn't involve marriage or spending too much time together. Then Orlando could get on with his life and Isobel could get on with hers and the hideous torment of this unrequited love would be banished to the dark recesses of her mind for ever.

Perhaps they could start with the fact that neither of them had felt able to go through with the wedding. What exactly did *that* say about their relationship? The wedding that, Isobel suddenly remembered with a jolt of alarm, fifty or so guests were still down there waiting to celebrate. Someone was going to have to make an announcement. And presumably that someone was her.

Gingerly looking over the battlements, Isobel pictured herself walking down the aisle between the rows of chairs in her beautiful wedding dress, every concerned face turned toward as she took her position under the rose-covered bower and explained, in her very best, most stiff-upper-lipped English, that there wouldn't actually be a wedding, but that she thanked them so much for coming and she did hope they hadn't been too inconvenienced.

It had to be done.

She was just about to turn to go down when the flash of a dark figure caught her eye—Orlando! He had appeared from nowhere, stepping out of the shadows cast by the walls of the *castello* and marching towards the lake, towards the assembled crowd, his stride fast and aggressive—panicked, even. She saw the way he ignored the guests as they turned to look at him, saw him finally stopping when he reached the front row, bending to speak to someone then straightening up, placing his hands on his hips, casting his gaze around.

Even from this distance she could see his agitation. He looked wild, unkempt and dangerously close to losing control: unlike Isobel had ever seen him before. Gone was the cool, composed Orlando she'd thought she knew, to be replaced with this thunderingly dark force of nature.

Oh, Orlando! Isobel felt her heart clench violently in her chest. She longed to go to him, fighting every instinct to stop herself from snatching up her skirts and running across the grass to join him, humiliating herself by begging him to marry her after all, begging him to love her.

Standing on tiptoes, she leant further over the battlements, trying to see his face, to work out what was going on beneath the rigidly held dark figure. But he was too far away, no matter how hard she strained her eyes, how far she reached forward.

Suddenly Orlando's head jerked up, his eyes flying in her direction, making Isobel start. She clutched at the crumbling stonework for support. A chunk of it came away in her hand, then hurtled towards the ground, followed by another, and then a third piece as the ancient stones dislodged each other and a section of the battlements started to fall apart before her eyes.

With a jolt of fear Isobel retreated several steps backwards, to the safety of the solid flagstones, and waited for her heart rate to steady—from the fright of her narrow escape but even more from the sight of Orlando.

Had he seen her? She couldn't be sure. But within a few minutes she knew the answer, when she heard her name being hoarsely yelled, accompanied by the pounding of footsteps and the rasping of breath as, ducking under the arched doorway, he appeared before her, tall and all-powerful and glowering with murderous intent.

'Isobel!'

She stood rooted to the spot as he marched towards her, encircling her with his strong arms, crushing her against his body. Isobel could feel his heart thudding against her cheek, his chest rising and falling with the force of each lungful of air. She closed her eyes, letting herself be held in his arms. Just for a moment.

'Are you okay? You're not hurt?' Pulling away enough to see her face, Orlando stared down at her, his pupils dilating, his eyes shining black.

'I'm fine.' Isobel moved within the circle of his arms but the band only tightened further.

'*Dio*, Isobel. You could have been killed.' Hugging her to him, he spoke over the top of her head, relief catching at his voice before it was swiftly replaced with harsh interrogation. 'What is the meaning of this anyway?' Pulling away again, he held Isobel at arm's length to glare into her eyes. 'What the hell are you doing up here?'

Stiffening her spine, Isobel tried to push him away with hands that trembled against the wall of his chest. 'I needed some space, some time to think.'

'Think about what?' He let his arms fall by his sides but his piercing stare never left her face.

'Lots of things. Why you didn't turn up for our wedding, for one.'

'What are you talking about? I'm here, aren't I?

'It's too late, Orlando.'

'Too late? What do you mean, too late?' Anger danced in his eyes, glinting like polished stone. 'Look, Isobel…'

Isobel watched him trying to rein in his temper, trying to appear reasonable—an effort that had him clenching his jaw, sharpening the angles of his face. 'If you feel you need to make a stand because I'm late then fair enough—point taken. I apologise. Now, can we just…?'

'No, Orlando. It's too late because I have realised that I can't go through with it. I can't marry you.'

Orlando's eyes narrowed to dangerous slits of fire.

'What do you mean, you can't go through with it? We agreed. It's all arranged.'

Isobel took a couple of steps away from him. The wind was getting stronger now, ruffling Orlando's dark curls, billowing inside his shirt that was half untucked from his jeans. It blew against the skirts of her dress, lifting the silky fabric, then moulding it against the length of her legs.

'I'm sorry, Orlando.'

'Sorry?' Taking a step towards her, Orlando cupped her bare shoulders with powerful hands that held her rigid beneath his grasp. 'I don't know what this is all about, Isobel, but I suggest you pull yourself together, right now, so that we can go down there and get this done.'

Isobel swallowed past the agonising lump in her throat, blinked against the tears that were scalding the backs of her eyes. *Get this done.* His callous phrase epitomised everything this marriage meant to him—everything *she* meant to him. She raked her eyes over the harsh contours of his beautiful face; he was cold, calculating and utterly ruthless. How had she ever thought she could marry a man with the power to hurt her so much?

'I'm sorry, Orlando.'

It really was all she could think of to say. Shrugging his hands off her shoulders, she went to move past him but he caught hold of them again, whipping her round to face him.

'And that's it, is it? All the explanation I'm going to get?' Fury contorted his features, scoured his voice. 'Do you *really* think I'm going to just accept that—let you walk away? I need a reason, Isobel. And I want to hear it right now.'

Isobel gazed back at him, strands of her hair blowing across her face, catching on her eyelashes, snagging against her dry lips. When she said nothing he increased the pressure on her shoulders, the warmth of his grip searing into her. *A reason.* He made it sound easy. Maybe it was easy. Maybe it was time to tell it as it was.

'Very well.' Biting down on her trembling lip, she raised her eyes, determined at least that she would meet his gaze full-on. 'I can't go through with the ceremony. I can't stand there and make my vows in front of those people knowing that the whole thing is nothing more than a sham.'

'It is no such thing. I intend to make a full commitment and honour my vows. And I expect you to do the same.'

'This is not about commitment or honour, Orlando.'

'So what *is* it about? Tell me.'

Orlando was leaning in so close to her now his face blurred out of focus. His breath was hot on her face.

'It's about love.' The words fell softly from her lips.

'Love?' He repeated the word with distaste. 'So

what are you saying? That you can't marry me because you don't love me?'

'No, Orlando.' Isobel drew in a breath as if it were her last. 'I'm saying I can't marry you because I do.'

CHAPTER TWELVE

ORLANDO STARED AT Isobel's upturned face, so stunningly beautiful, but haunted with an anguish that flayed his skin.

She loved him? Had he known? No. Because he had refused to go there—refused to open up the hard kernel of his heart to the possibility. The same way he had refused to examine his feelings for her.

'Let me get this straight.'

He heard himself being cold, harsh, authoritative. *Being a jerk.* He realised he was still gripping Isobel's shoulders—too hard. Releasing them, he clasped his hands behind his back, watching the pink marks on her skin fade back to creamy white.

'You won't marry me because you *love* me.'

He tried to phrase it as if she was being wildly irrational, as if she was the mad one here. But even as he barked the words he knew. He knew exactly what he was saying.

Isobel gave him a long stare, her throat moving in a painful swallow.

'You have to try and understand, Orlando. I *can't* marry you because you don't love me. It simply wouldn't be right.'

'Love!' He deliberately imbued the word with pitiful derision. And he hated himself for it. 'Where

has this come from? Since when has *love* been part of this arrangement?'

He saw Isobel's lower lip quiver, felt the nip as she bit down hard on it as surely as if she had bitten his own.

'I don't know.' The words trembled. 'I suppose since I first realised I was in love with you.'

Orlando felt the pain of her confession sear through him, stabbing him with a thousand knives, and he had to turn away. He couldn't bear to look into those green eyes any longer.

'Believe me, you wouldn't want my love even if it was there to give.' He lowered his voice, fighting to control his emotions. 'Love brings nothing but pain and sorrow.'

Quiet wrapped itself around them, blocking out the faint strains of chatter and music from far below, the crack of the flag above their heads.

'Why do you say that?'

Isobel's softly spoken question turned him back to face her again.

'Because it's true. Love has the power to destroy like nothing else. I should know. I watched it destroying my mother. Her life was doomed from the moment she had the misfortune to fall in love with my father.'

'But it doesn't have to always be like that.' Isobel challenged him softly, a tremor of tragic desperation in her voice.

'And love destroyed Sophia.' Orlando cruelly dismissed her words.

'Sophia?' Isobel repeated her name with a quiet jolt of surprise. 'The girl who died in the fire in the warehouse?'

'*Sì.* Sophia—who died because of me.'

'I don't understand.'

Orlando raked in a breath. Caught in the spell of Isobel's clear green eyes, he was astonished to find himself teetering on the brink of telling her. *No.* He pulled himself back. Why would he do that? Why would he want to humiliate himself, betray his weakness, expose the miserable raw underbelly of his life? And to Isobel of all people.

And yet... Still she gazed up at him, silently waiting, a patch of blue sky reflected in the sheen of her eyes. Maybe she deserved to know the truth. Maybe she deserved to know exactly the sort of man she had so foolishly fallen in love with.

'Sophia and I were lovers.' He saw her flinch at his words but there was no going back now. 'We used to meet in the warehouse. It was our secret place.' He spoke in choppy sentences, as if trying to protect Isobel from the pain he had carried around for so long. It was pure masochism that drove him on, forced him to continue as he took in Isobel's look of stunned horror. 'We had arranged to meet there the night of the fire—the night my father torched the place. I knew she was waiting for me.'

Her eyes glittering with the sheen of tears, Isobel gave an almost imperceptible nod.

'Obviously I had no idea that my father would carry out his hideous plan that very night.' With brutal frankness, Orlando carried on. 'But that doesn't mean I wasn't to blame. Sophia wouldn't have been there if it hadn't been for me.'

As Isobel went to speak he raised a hand to silence her.

'Wait. There is more to this wretched tale. After Sophia's body was taken away I went back to the *castello*—I had nowhere else to go. My father was there—drunk, celebrating his success. I just about managed to hang on to my sanity long enough to tell him what he had done—that Sophia had been in the warehouse, that she was dead—and then I lost it completely. I knocked him to the ground, started battering him with my fists. I would have killed him, Isobel, I know I would—battered him to death on the floor of the drawing room in this very *castello* if I hadn't been stopped. Luckily for him, the police turned up.

'I spent the night in the cells. Meanwhile my father made a statement, stating that *I* was responsible for the fire, for Sophia's death. He said he didn't know how or why—sheer carelessness, a lovers' tiff maybe. His son was prone to fits of violent temper after all. Hadn't the police witnessed the brutal attack he had made on his own father? No doubt he had inherited the mental health issues that had plagued his mother all her life.'

'Oh, Orlando.' Isobel let out a plaintive cry. 'How could he be so cruel?'

'Despite his best efforts to frame me, my father's despicable reputation meant that the police were suspicious. I was fortunate. A witness came forward to say they had seen him entering the warehouse before the blaze started, traces of paraffin were found on his clothing and he was charged the next day. I was free to go. And that's what I did—I fled.

'Instead of paying my respects to Sophia's parents, throwing myself on their mercy and begging their forgiveness, I ran away. While they were preparing to lay their daughter to rest I was plotting my escape. On the day of her funeral, when I should have been there, facing the family around her graveside, saying my last goodbye to Sophia, I was on an aeroplane to New York. It was an act of cowardice that I will never forgive myself for.

'And do you want to know the worst of it, Isobel? Do you want to know the sort of man I really am?' Raking a hand through his windblown hair, he held her eyes with blistering intensity. 'The money for that one-way ticket to a new life—where do you think it came from? That's right. It was the money

my father had given me to burn down the warehouse. Blood money.'

There—it was said. The truth was finally told.

With the shame of his heinous past pumping
violently through his veins Orlando waited for
Isobel to recoil in horror, to see him as he saw himself. Not just responsible for the death of a young
woman, but a miserable coward who had never
faced up to his crime—a beast capable of such vio-
lence that he might have beaten his father to death
and a miserable lowlife to boot, depraved enough
to use blood money for his own gain.

In short, he was his father's son.

He watched the shiver sweep across Isobel's skin
as his miserable confession bedded in. Her slim
shoulders were twitching, her chest rising with
each short breath, pushing the swell of her breasts
over the tight-fitting bodice. He had never seen
her look more beautiful. He had never wanted her
more. He had never felt so destroyed.

'I'm so sorry, Orlando.' Tears were falling now,
from the well of her green eyes, sliding silently and
unchecked down her cheeks. 'That must have been
the most horrendous experience for you.'

Orlando glowered at her, uncomprehending.

'But thank you for telling me.' With a loud sniff
Isobel gathered up her skirts and made as if to
move.

'Is that it?' Reaching out, Orlando placed his

hands on her hips, halting her movement. 'Is that all you have to say? At least give me the satisfaction of showing me the disgust that I deserve.'

'Disgust?' Pinned to the spot, Isobel raised her eyes to his. 'No, not disgust—never that. You were a young man who had just suffered the most tragic bereavement, whose world had collapsed. You were frightened and alone, and desperation makes us all do stupid things.' She lowered her gaze, the sweep of her lashes dark with tears. 'But at least now I see why you could never love me or anyone else. When Sophia died you lost your one and only true love.'

Sophia? His true love? Sure, she had been his *first* love. With a heady, all-consuming rush of hormones and lust he had fallen hard for the pretty wine merchant's daughter. But his one and only love? No, not like that—not the way Isobel meant it. His love for Sophia had been replaced with an abiding guilt the moment he had held her lifeless body in his arms.

'Had I known, I would never have confessed my love for you.' Isobel was still talking, her cheeks wet with the tracks of her tears. 'It was stupid. I'm sorry. The last thing you need is the burden of that.'

'It's not a burden.'

'I would take it back if I could.'

'I don't want you to take it back.'

Suddenly Orlando knew that with absolute certainty. With a fierce conviction that drove through him like a sword.

'I have to go now.'

'No!'

'I need to change out of this dress.'

Isobel looked down as if seeing herself for the first time. She spoke slowly, deliberately, with the kind of voice one might use to stop someone throwing themselves off a bridge. Or indeed a medieval battlement.

'You should go and tell everyone that the wedding is off.'

Turning away, she started towards the doorway but Orlando was too quick for her, moving with lightning speed to block the door with his towering body.

'No, Isobel, I will do no such thing.'

'Then I'll do it myself.' Isobel stared at him coldly now, brushing the tears away with the back of her hand. Her mood had shifted, hardened, as if her pain had solidified. 'Because I can never marry you knowing that you love someone else. Even if, tragically, she is no longer alive.'

'I am *not* still in love with Sophia!' The words roared from somewhere deep inside him.

'No?' Isobel blinked against the force of his statement. 'Well, it makes no difference. Because you can obviously never love *me*. I have to try and protect myself, Orlando. My decision still stands.'

'*Dio*, Isobel.' Orlando reached towards her, his palms upward in a gesture of tormented frustration. 'Don't you see I am trying to protect you too? The reason I can't give you my love is not because it died along with Sophia. It's because my love is nothing but a poisoned chalice—a dreadful curse for those I inflict it upon.'

Isobel shook her head. 'No, Orlando, that's just an excuse. The real reason is because you have no love to give. Not to me, anyway.'

'That's not true.'

'Because if you loved me the way I love you, you wouldn't be able to deny it—no matter what the repercussions might be. Believe me, I know—because I've tried. And still I find myself standing here before you, making an utter fool of myself—'

Her voice cracked into silence.

'No, Isobel.' Closing the space between them, Orlando caught her in his arms but she twisted away, stepping back. 'Not a fool. Never that. You are smart and beautiful and brave.'

And, despite the way I have treated you, you are in love with me. How could that be?

'Please don't say any more.' Moving towards him again, Isobel placed her fingertips to his lips, halting his words. 'You are just making it hurt all the more.'

It was a gesture so gentle, so loving, that Orlando felt every muscle in his body turn to lead.

Isobel loved him. And what was he doing? Instead of embracing her love he was rejecting it— no, worse—punishing her for it.

Removing her hand, Orlando held it against his heart, pressing it firmly against the pounding beat. A strange stillness came over him. Suddenly he was in the calm centre of the turning world, where nothing mattered except this moment. Just him and Isobel. For once he was solely in the present. Somewhere he had never allowed himself to linger before, always so busy planning for the future or trying unsuccessfully to erase his past.

When Isobel had told him she was pregnant he had gone flying headlong into full control mode, never stopping to consider her feelings—never stopping to consider his own. At no time had he let himself stand still and just *be. Feel.* The way he was doing now.

Now it was as if Isobel had slammed the brakes on his frantic, self-absorbed life. Made him open his eyes to see that all his assumptions about life, and about love, had been coloured by the veil of his past. Isobel had lifted that veil and left him staring at what lay beneath.

And what had he found?

That confessing his shameful past *hadn't* ripped open the wounds of guilt. It had been painful, yes, and certainly his abiding sadness for the tragic loss of a young life would never leave him. But

Isobel's compassion, her gentle intuitive insight, had made him see that maybe it was time he cut himself some slack.

What was it she had said? *You were frightened and alone*. He had certainly been that.

All these years he'd thought he had been escaping his past—eradicating the father he hated so much, burying his own crimes deep in his subconscious—when actually he had been doing no such thing. He had been letting it consume him. He had been blinded by it, using it as an excuse to deny his Italian roots, to turn his back on his heritage. Now, by confessing to Isobel, he had unlocked his self-imposed shackles and to his surprise, rather than loathing him for his crimes, she had shown him a tender acceptance that had finally lifted the burden.

But there was another naked truth that Orlando had to face up to. Another shameful realisation. Now he knew that by holding Isobel at arm's length, denying his feelings for her, shunning her declaration of love, he hadn't been protecting her. He had been protecting *himself*. And that sickening thought struck him like a physical blow.

He had to put things right. Life was about *now*. He had this one precious moment. And if he didn't grab it, hold on tight and make it count, he would never, *ever* forgive himself.

The wind had suddenly dropped, the flag above

them drooping to silence. The world was holding its breath. Waiting.

Tipping Isobel's chin to gaze at her face, Orlando finally let himself fall. Deeper and deeper, plunging headlong into the swirling abyss of her sea-green eyes. This time he wasn't going to stop himself, wasn't going to put out a hand to break his fall. This time he was going to let himself drop into the unknown, scary, wonderful chasm of love.

For he knew now with an all-consuming certainty that he loved Isobel. That he had most probably loved her from the very first moment he had seen her wobbling to stand up on the boat, when he had taken her hand in his. The very hand he held to his chest now. Pride, obstinacy and downright fear had made him deny it, refused to let him see it. But by declaring her love for him, forcing him to open up to her, Isobel had set him free.

Brave, beautiful, honourable Isobel. She had released him to love her in the way he had always wanted to do. The way he should have done from the start.

Now he just had to tell her.

Dragging in a breath that shook his body, he felt the weight of his love welling up inside him, flowing from a stream to a torrent to a deluge, until the words he had never said couldn't be held in any longer, spewing from his body, from his very soul.

'I love you, Isobel.'

There—it was said. The relief was enormous, as if a boulder had been lifted from his shoulders. He watched the look of shock that widened Isobel's eyes: shock mingled with uncertainty, mingled with hope.

'Orlando…'

'I love you, Isobel.' He would say it as many times as he had to.

'But you can't. I mean, not after everything you have said…'

'I love you, Isobel.'

Suddenly he knew there was only way to show Isobel that he meant it. Really, *really* meant it.

Cupping her chin in his hands, he lowered his head, breathing deeply, relishing the split second of delirium before he claimed her lips. They felt so soft under his own, so warm and plump, so delectably, tantalisingly wonderful that Orlando immediately started to tremble. His hands were shaking against Isobel's skin with the effort of controlling himself, holding back the rocketing desire that was commanding him to take her, right here and now. To prove his love to her in the most carnal way possible.

Later, he told himself. Later he would make love to her and it would be the sweetest, most wonderful experience of his life. Of Isobel's too, if he had any say in it. But right now he would have to content himself with a kiss.

As Isobel started to respond he moved his hands behind her head, threading his fingers through her hair, dislodging one of the roses in order to pull her closer. Sliding his tongue between her lips, he felt her open up to him, her breath hot and sweet, making his heart sing with joy and relief. And when she wrapped her bare arms around his neck, pressing her soft body against his to deepen their kiss, he heard himself groan his pleasure.

His tongue sought hers now, tasting her, touching her, his lips gently rocking over hers in a rhythmic, pulsating pressure that he wouldn't stop until he was sure he had stolen away her doubts. Sure that she was his.

Hearing Isobel's sigh of pleasure, feeling the way she moulded herself against him, he finally gave himself permission to believe, to move his hands down to cup her bottom through the silky fabric of her dress, permission to press the hard length of himself against her. *Dio*, she felt so good!

Releasing her lips, he trailed soft kisses down the length of her exposed neck, feeling her judder beneath him until he stopped at the base of her neck, where he rasped his tongue against the shadowed hollow. Then, judging that it was time, he raised his eyes to find hers.

Eyes closed, head thrown back against the ecstasy of his kisses, Isobel let her body surrender to Orlando, let her mind close down completely.

She couldn't think. She didn't want to think. She just wanted to be here, in this moment, for ever. Orlando's tender, loving touch had spread through her body, melting her bones like butter, awakening her desire and reaffirming her love for him. For now, that was enough.

The shock of his heartbreaking confession had left her lungs burning for air. Not because of what he'd done—her heart had gone out to the seventeen-year-old for the terrible plight he had found himself in. But because of the pain she had seen in his eyes as he had relived his ordeal, the torment and despair that she now knew had followed in his footsteps, no matter how far he had run, how many thousands of miles he had put between himself and Trevente, the place that had seen such suffering.

Now she understood why he had been so resistant to take the title of Marchese di Trevente, why he had loathed the *castello* so much when they had first visited it that sunlit spring evening. She understood too, what it must have cost him to come back here to face his demons in order to make this place his home. *Their home.* Somewhere they could raise their child, be a family. He had done that for her.

Because he loved her? Could she really believe that?

Despite the glorious drag of his lips against her skin, the damp heat of his tongue that was driving her crazy with longing, the doubts started to creep back in. Was it really possible that opening up to her about his past had finally allowed Orlando to love again? To love *her*?

Now, as if to compound her doubts, he had stopped the glorious attention he had been paying to her angled neck. Slowly opening eyes drugged with desire, she realised that Orlando was staring at her, watching her with such rapt concentration it was as if he was trying to look into her very soul.

Isobel blinked, then gazed back. She had no chance of doing anything else, pulled as she was by the power of Orlando's force like the ocean tide by the moon. But what she saw there stole the breath from her chest, stopped her heart in mid-beat. Because now she knew it was for real. Shining deep in the ebony darkness of his beautiful eyes was the unmistakable, undeniable declaration of love.

'Come here.'

Pulling her towards him again, Orlando splayed his strong hands around her waist, bending her backwards so that she arched provocatively against him.

They were in the master bedroom, Orlando having scooped Isobel up in his arms and negotiated the steps down from the tower, with her laughing and crying and clinging on to him as if she would never let go. Despite Orlando insisting she was utterly beautiful, she had told him she needed to rescue the mess of her hairstyle and sort out her streaked make-up while he changed into his wedding outfit.

'Let's just skip the wedding and go straight to bed.'

He was leaning over her now, nuzzling her neck, blatantly trying to seduce her.

'No, Orlando!' Laughing, Isobel raised her hands to his bare shoulders, pushing him back. 'Wedding first…wedding night afterwards. Those are the rules.'

Orlando groaned. 'Rules, bossing me about, denying me the delights of your flesh… Is this what married life is going to be like with you?' He tucked a strand of hair behind Isobel's ear. 'You know the longer you make me wait, the longer I will have to spend making love to you when the time comes?'

Isobel lips curved into a seductive smile. 'Is that so? I guess that is a penance I will have to endure.'

'Hmm…too right. I've a good mind to make you start enduring it right now.'

His fingers strayed to the outline of her suspenders through the silky fabric of her dress, but Isobel removed his hands and pressed his fingertips to her lips.

'Later, Orlando.'

It was a promise loaded with such intent that Orlando could only groan again, with a sexual hunger that Isobel felt ripple to the core of her being.

Planting a kiss on her lips, he finally let her go and moved over to the wardrobe. Unable to stop her eyes from following him, Isobel drank in the sight of his lean, muscular body, clad only in a pair of snug white boxers. Those taut buttocks were still holding her attention when he turned round, his suit over his arm and a wicked glint in his eye.

'You keep looking at me like that, Ms Spicer, and we are *never* going to get to this wedding.'

'Get dressed, soon-to-be-husband. We've kept those poor people waiting long enough, don't you think?'

'*E vero*. That's true.' Buttoning up his shirt, Orlando gazed at her, his dark eyes burning with passion, brimming with love. 'But you are sure you want to go through with this now? We could plan something else—a bigger wedding or a smaller one. St Paul's Cathedral. The Plaza, New York. The top of the Himalayas if that's what you'd like. Just say the word and it shall be yours.'

'Tempting though that is, I am happy with this wedding.' Moving to stand in front of him, Isobel took the grey silk tie from his hand and, turning up his shirt collar, carefully looped it around his neck and fashioned an expert knot. 'Very happy, in fact. I'm sure it will be perfect.'

'I'm sure too.' Leaning forward, Orlando kissed

her again, then took both her hands in his. 'Thank you so much, Isobel, for making me see sense. For believing in me. I'm going to make you very happy, I promise—you *and* our child.'

'You already do.' Pulling away one hand, she brushed a stray tear from her eyelashes, then placed her hand on her tummy. 'And I am speaking for both of us.'

He covered her hand with his own and Isobel felt his warmth spreading right through her.

'Then I thank both of you from the bottom of my heart. *Grazie mille.*' He kissed her once more. 'Come on, then, my beautiful bride.' Pulling on his jacket and adjusting the cuffs, he stood back to gaze at Isobel. 'If you are ready, let's do this.'

Isobel nodded, not trusting herself to speak as she took his outstretched hand in hers. But one thing she knew—she had never been more ready for anything in her life.

The chattering died down, turning to hushed whispers as the wedding guests realised that the bride and groom were finally here. Standing at the top of the grassy aisle, Orlando and Isobel stood side by side, Isobel's arm linked through Orlando's, their bodies less than a confetti flake apart.

The officiant took his place and as the string quartet started to play Orlando and Isobel moved forward, between the rows of chairs, towards the sparkling lake and the rose-covered bower, to the ceremony that would bind them together for ever.

Admittedly it wasn't the traditional way to do it. But, walking beside Orlando, Isobel felt nothing but joy. She was marrying the man she loved, and miraculously he loved her too. That was all that mattered.

As they reached the front Elena darted forward to give Isobel the bouquet that she had completely forgotten about, and then bent down to arrange the folds of her dress. Smiling her thanks, Isobel let her eyes slide to the side—and there they halted in astonishment. Because seated next to Maria, with an empty champagne glass in one hand and a walking stick in the other, was none other than her mother!

'About time too.' Imperiously handing the glass to Maria, Nancy Spicer started to rise to her feet. 'I was starting to think this wedding was never going to happen.'

'Mother!' Isobel stared at her in utter amazement. 'What are you doing here?'

'What does it look like I'm doing?' She was leaning heavily on her stick and it started to wobble beneath her, but Orlando was there, a steadying arm under her elbow. 'I've come to give my daughter away at her wedding. Thank you, young man.' She turned to Orlando, giving him a tipsy smile.

'Give me away? But you said...'

'Never mind what I said. Now, if we could all just get into position, I will be fine to stand alone from now on.'

'You will?' Isobel swung her incredulous gaze to Orlando, who shrugged his shoulders in mock surprise.

'There.' Feet firmly planted, Mrs Spicer haughtily raised her chin. 'I am ready now.'

'You look amazing, Mum!' Leaning across, Isobel kissed her mother's cheek. 'Thank you so much for coming. I can't tell you what it means to have you here.'

'Nonsense.' Bright pink spots of pleasure appeared beneath her powdered cheeks. 'If you want to thank anyone, thank that young man of yours. This is all *his* doing.'

'Is it, indeed?'

Isobel slanted at look at Orlando, who was still busy feigning innocence. Standing on tiptoe, she cupped his chin, silently mouthing the words *thank you* before kissing him lightly on the lips.

You're very welcome. He mouthed the words back, his eyes shining with love.

'Come on, then.' Nancy Spicer waved her stick impatiently. 'Is this wedding going to take place or not?'

'It is, Nancy.' Pulling Isobel closer to his side, Orlando took hold of her hand and raised it to his lips. 'It's going to take place right now. Because

I don't want to have to wait a moment longer to marry your daughter. Isobel is the most beautiful, wonderful and amazing person I have ever known. And I love her more than words can say.'

EPILOGUE

THE MOTORBOAT CHUGGED steadily across the turquoise sea towards the island of Jacamar.

'Signor Orlando!' A smiling, deeply tanned man deftly caught the rope that Orlando threw to him. 'Welcome back to Jacamar. It's been too long.'

'*Grazie*, Miguel.' Jumping ashore Orlando warmly embraced his island manager. 'How have things been here?'

'Oh, you know— pretty chilled.'

'That's what I like to hear.' Orlando gave him a cheerful slap on the back.

'I can see you have a very precious cargo there.' Shielding his eyes from the sun, Miguel surveyed the occupants of the boat.

'I do indeed.' Orlando stretched out a hand to his mother-in-law. 'Nancy, if you would like to get out first? Miguel, allow me to introduce my mother-in-law, Mrs Spicer. Perhaps if we could both help her ashore…?'

'Don't fuss. I'm perfectly capable of getting out of a boat.' Despite her protestations Nancy allowed herself to be lifted like a featherweight onto dry land by the strong arms of the two men. 'And be careful with my luggage. I don't want you dropping my suitcase into the sea.'

'No, ma'am.' Miguel gave a respectful bow.

'And I think you know my wife, don't you, Miguel?'

'I do so! Hello there, Ms Spicer… I mean Signora Cassano…'

'Isobel!' Laughing, Isobel waved to him as she prepared to get off the boat. 'Hi, Miguel. Great to see you again.'

'And who, may I ask, is *this*?'

Grinning broadly, Miguel looked down at the squirming bundle being held tightly in Isobel's arms.

'Say hello to Nico!' Isobel moved towards the side of the boat. 'Something tells me he is keen to come ashore!'

'Come on, then, young man.' Squatting down, Orlando reached for his son as Isobel held him aloft.

Shooting out his chubby arms, little Nico gave a shriek of excitement as his father grasped him, swinging him high in the air before settling him comfortably on his hip.

The boat rocked gently as Orlando held out his free hand to Isobel and their eyes met. A vivid flash of recognition shot between them. Everything that had happened in the turbulent months since they had last done this was encapsulated in their clasped hands now.

It seemed impossible to Isobel that it had only been just over a year ago. So much had happened. Everything had changed. But with the happiest possible ending.

A secret smile passed between them and, giving her hand an extra squeeze, Orlando helped her ashore.

'This holiday was a great idea.' She linked arms with her husband and the small party slowly made their way along the pathway through the lush greenery towards the main house. 'You were right—we all need a break.'

'You more than anyone. Life has been pretty hectic lately, what with the baby and Spicer Shoes and everything. You *do* know how proud I am of you, don't you, Isobel? The way your business has taken off has been phenomenal.'

'Thank you. But I couldn't have done it without you.'

'We make a good team, that's for sure—even if you *did* take some convincing. I seem to remember a time when you couldn't wait to buy back the Cassano Holdings shares.'

Isobel pulled a face at his teasing. 'Sorry. I *was* a bit stroppy.'

'I won't argue with that!'

'Anyway.' Isobel opted for a quick change of

subject. 'I am so proud of you too. The Trevente estate has been transformed. Seeing it providing homes and secure employment for all those people is fantastic. And just think—now that the vineyards are being properly tended we should be able to start producing wine again next year.'

'*Sì*. And then we will raise a glass to us—to our family and the future.'

'And maybe we'll have a moment's silence for Sophia too.' Isobel gave him a tender look.

'*Sì,*' Orlando repeated quietly. 'We will do that. Meanwhile, I think it's fair to say we are both pretty proud of this one.' Taking hold of one of Nico's bare feet, Orlando bounced him on his hip. 'It's only right that we have brought him back here, to show him where he came from.'

'Well, maybe we'll skip that bit in front of my mother.' Isobel laughed.

'She wouldn't care. She clearly adores him.'

'She does, doesn't she? She's a changed woman, Orlando, and I know I have you to thank for that. Even though I have no idea what you said or did to bring about this transformation.'

'Aha.' Orlando tapped the side of his nose. 'We just had a little chat. You should know by now that you Spicer women can't resist my charms.'

'It's true—I can't even deny it.' Isobel grinned up at him. 'And that's despite the growing swell of your head. Well, whatever you said, I thank you. The change has been amazing. Just look at her now.'

They both watched Nancy, striding along the pathway ahead of them, leaning on Miguel's arm—the better to be able to chat to him, rather than for any actual support.

'And you really don't mind her coming to live at the *castello*?'

'Mind?' Orlando turned to look at her, wicked innocence dancing in his eyes. 'Why would I mind? I have always found her to be perfectly charming.'

'Yeah, right.' Isobel gave him a dig in the ribs. 'Seriously, though, I do wish *your* mother could have been here to see Nico.' She sighed wistfully.

'So do I.' Stopping on the pathway, Orlando turned and gazed at her. 'I know she would have loved him. And loved you too. But now's not the time for regrets, Isobel. Now is the time to be thankful for all that we have. Because, believe me, I am truly, *truly* thankful.'

'Oh, Orlando.' Raising her arms, Isobel hooked them around Orlando's neck and drew him close to whisper against his ear. 'Me too.'

Their lips met, swiftly moving into a passionate kiss that was rudely interrupted by a squawk and a determined wriggle from the small body trapped between them.

'*Scusi*, Nico.' Pulling away, Orlando dropped

a kiss on the top of his head. 'Forgive me. I was just showing your *mamma* how much I love her.'

And with that the three of them started walking again, towards the house and the future and a lifetime of happiness.

* * * * *

LARGER-PRINT BOOKS!

GET 2 FREE LARGER-PRINT NOVELS PLUS
2 FREE GIFTS!

HARLEQUIN

Romance

From the Heart, For the Heart

LARGER-PRINT BOOKS!
GET 2 FREE LARGER-PRINT NOVELS PLUS
2 FREE GIFTS!

HARLEQUIN

super romance®

More Story...More Romance

YES! Please send me 2 FREE LARGER-PRINT Harlequin® Superromance® novels and my 2 FREE gifts (gifts are worth about $10). After receiving them, if I don't wish to receive any more books, I can return the shipping statement marked "cancel." If I don't cancel, I will receive 4 brand-new novels every month and be billed just $5.94 per book in the U.S. or $6.24 per book in Canada. That's a savings of at least 12% off the cover price! It's quite a bargain! Shipping and handling is just 50¢ per book in the U.S. or 75¢ per book in Canada.* I understand that accepting the 2 free books and gifts places me under no obligation to buy anything. I can always return a shipment and cancel at any time. Even if I never buy another book, the two free books and gifts are mine to keep forever.

132/332 HDN GHVC

Name _____ (PLEASE PRINT)

Address _____ Apt. #

City _____ State/Prov. _____ Zip/Postal Code

Signature (if under 18, a parent or guardian must sign)

Mail to the **Reader Service:**
IN U.S.A.: P.O. Box 1867, Buffalo, NY 14240-1867
IN CANADA: P.O. Box 609, Fort Erie, Ontario L2A 5X3

Want to try two free books from another line?
Call 1-800-873-8635 today or visit www.ReaderService.com.

* Terms and prices subject to change without notice. Prices do not include applicable taxes. Sales tax applicable in N.Y. Canadian residents will be charged applicable taxes. Offer not valid in Quebec. This offer is limited to one order per household. Not valid for current subscribers to Harlequin Superromance Larger-Print books. All orders subject to credit approval. Credit or debit balances in a customer's account(s) may be offset by any other outstanding balance owed by or to the customer. Please allow 4 to 6 weeks for delivery. Offer available while quantities last.

Your Privacy—The Reader Service is committed to protecting your privacy. Our Privacy Policy is available online at www.ReaderService.com or upon request from the Reader Service.

We make a portion of our mailing list available to reputable third parties that offer products we believe may interest you. If you prefer that we not exchange your name with third parties, or if you wish to clarify or modify your communication preferences, please visit us at www.ReaderService.com/consumerchoice or write to us at Reader Service Preference Service, P.O. Box 9062, Buffalo, NY 14240-9062. Include your complete name and address.

HSRLP15

LARGER-PRINT BOOKS!
GET 2 FREE LARGER-PRINT NOVELS PLUS
2 FREE GIFTS!

HARLEQUIN®

INTRIGUE
BREATHTAKING ROMANTIC SUSPENSE

YES! Please send me 2 FREE LARGER-PRINT Harlequin® Intrigue novels and my 2 FREE gifts (gifts are worth about $10). After receiving them, if I don't wish to receive any more books, I can return the shipping statement marked "cancel." If I don't cancel, I will receive 6 brand-new novels every month and be billed just $5.49 per book in the U.S. or $6.24 per book in Canada. That's a saving of at least 11% off the cover price! It's quite a bargain! Shipping and handling is just 50¢ per book in the U.S. and 75¢ per book in Canada.* I understand that accepting the 2 free books and gifts places me under no obligation to buy anything. I can always return a shipment and cancel at any time. Even if I never buy another book, the two free books and gifts are mine to keep forever.

199/399 HDN GHWN

Name _____ (PLEASE PRINT) _____

Address _____ Apt. # _____

City _____ State/Prov. _____ Zip/Postal Code _____

Signature (if under 18, a parent or guardian must sign) _____

Mail to the Reader Service:
IN U.S.A.: P.O. Box 1867, Buffalo, NY 14240-1867
IN CANADA: P.O. Box 609, Fort Erie, Ontario L2A 5X3

**Are you a subscriber to Harlequin® Intrigue books
and want to receive the larger-print edition?
Call 1-800-873-8635 today or visit www.ReaderService.com.**

* Terms and prices subject to change without notice. Prices do not include applicable taxes. Sales tax applicable in N.Y. Canadian residents will be charged applicable taxes. Offer not valid in Quebec. This offer is limited to one order per household. Not valid for current subscribers to Harlequin Intrigue Larger-Print books. All orders subject to credit approval. Credit or debit balances in a customer's account(s) may be offset by any other outstanding balance owed by or to the customer. Please allow 4 to 6 weeks for delivery. Offer available while quantities last.

Your Privacy—The Reader Service is committed to protecting your privacy. Our Privacy Policy is available online at www.ReaderService.com or upon request from the Reader Service.

We make a portion of our mailing list available to reputable third parties that offer products we believe may interest you. If you prefer that we not exchange your name with third parties, or if you wish to clarify or modify your communication preferences, please visit us at www.ReaderService.com/consumerchoice or write to us at Reader Service Preference Service, P.O. Box 9062, Buffalo, NY 14240-9062. Include your complete name and address.

HILP15

KSB